THE SPECIALISTS

Also by Lawrence Block available from
Carroll & Graf:

Such Men Are Dangerous

THE SPECIALISTS

LAWRENCE BLOCK

Carroll & Graf Publishers, Inc.
New York

For Bob Ferguson

Published by arrangement with the author and the author's agent, Knox Burger Associates, Inc.

First Carroll & Graf edition 1993

Carroll & Graf Publishers, Inc.
260 Fifth Avenue
New York, NY 10001

ISBN 0-7867-0046-7

Manufactured in the United States of America

THE SPECIALISTS

Before

Albert Platt looked better with clothes on. He had his suits made by an East Side tailor, his shoes by a London boot-maker, and his ties by a countess. With his clothes on and his hair combed and his jowls shaved and cologned, he looked like a successful hoodlum. Naked, he looked like a gorilla.

He was naked now. He sat on the edge of a high-backed Victorian wing chair in the living room of his suite at the Desert Palms. Glossy black hairs curled on his abdomen and chest. Sweat beaded on his forehead and under his arms.

In his right hand he held a .38-caliber revolver with a two-inch barrel. The gun was heavy, and Platt eased the load by resting his elbow on the arm of the chair. The muzzle of the gun just touched the center of the girl's forehead.

The girl was also naked, which was all she had in common with Platt. She was half his age and half his weight, a long-bodied redhead, trim of breasts and bottom and thighs. She knelt at Platt's feet like a supplicant at the rail.

"Two hundred bucks," Platt said. "Fifteen minutes, half an hour, two bills isn't bad, right? You just be a good girl and you can go buy yourself a Cadillac."

The girl heard the words but couldn't hold onto them. Nothing existed for her now but the mouth of the revolver. She had begun to perform as he had demanded, and the gun must have been lodged between the cushion and frame of the chair, because all at once it was in his hand and its cold metal mouth was touching her forehead and his voice was telling her that she would barely feel it at all, just one bright streak of pain and it would be over before she knew it.

"A gun goes off," Platt said. "In your forehead or in your mouth, your pretty mouth. A bang is a bang."

The girl was performing what journalists call an unnatural act. She had always wondered why it was so labeled, because it had never seemed anything other than natural to her. Until now.

"Like a baby with a bottle," Platt said. "Oh, be a good baby, that's a good baby. You don't want to die, baby. That's right, baby. You don't want to die, all that beautiful money, two hundred beautiful dollars, nobody wants to die, baby, you don't want to die."

An important man, they had told her downstairs. Donna, kid, this is an important gennulman, you want to treat him right. A banker, a very well-connected gennulman, his first trip to Vegas in three years, Donna, you want to make him real happy.

Oh, yes, she thought, yes, I want to make him happy. You better believe I want to make him happy. Oh, God, I want to get out of here. Two hundred beautiful dollars, fuck his beautiful dollars, I need it like a hole in the head. Oh, Jesus, a hole in the head—

An image flashed in her mind, a newspaper halftone, all dots, her face, with one huge black dot in the center of her forehead. A two-column cut with a headline over it and a few paragraphs below. Donna Mackenzie model and dancer found in the desert persons unknown funeral private.

"Oh," Platt said. "Oh. Oh. Ah, baby, baby, baby."

Don't run and retch, don't, don't. Just stay, just wait, and God make the gun go away, make it go away, make him be fair, his game and his rules, and God, God make him be fair.

"Sorry, baby," Platt said.

God, you cheated—

The trigger squeaked back. An eternal instant, a world of forever black.

The hammer clicked on an empty chamber.

Laughter, roaring, rolling, dying down. His footsteps across the deep carpet to the bedroom. The slam of the bedroom door.

She stood up. She spat on the carpet. She looked at the stain. There was a sudden rush of vertigo, as if the carpet were miles away. Her head swam, her knees buckled. She almost fell.

She pulled her dress over her head, grabbed up her underwear and stockings. She put on one shoe and couldn't find the other. She was looking around for it when she heard his laugh again from the other side of the bedroom door.

She kicked off the one shoe. The hell with the shoes. Her purse was on the lamp table and she snatched it with her free hand. The hell with the shoes, they were cheap shoes, she could buy other shoes. She had two hundred dollars in her purse, two hundred beautiful dollars that she would love to change into dimes and shove up his ass. Or make it pennies, the son of a bitch, the dirty son of a bitch.

She ran for the door.

One

Manso was shaving when someone started pounding on the door. He had a towel around his middle and a face half full of lather. He called out, "Yeah, just a minute," and brought the razor into position for another stroke.

The pounding didn't stop, and over it he heard Donna's voice. He was about to tell her to wait, but something in her tone changed his mind. He went to the door, still carrying the razor, still wearing the towel and the lather.

"I was just shaving," he told her. "I didn't expect . . . what's the matter?"

He had never seen her like this, face pale and drawn, eyes crazed, desperate. He started to say something, stopped himself, turned to lock the door. When he turned around again, she was climbing out of her dress.

He said, "Baby, I don't——" and her eyes flashed at him.

"Don't ever call me *baby*."

"Huh?"

She was suddenly gasping for breath. He stared at her. He had been in Vegas for three weeks and sleeping with her for two and he had never seen her like this. She wasn't a girl who got like this. She was bright eyes and laughter at the shows and cool reserve at the dice tables and friendly clean fire in bed. She was never hysteria; it didn't fit.

She said, "I took a shower, I used a mouthwash. I can't get clean. I took a shower so hot it burned. Eddie, please. I can't talk, I just can't. The shower was hot but I'm cold cold cold and I have to be warm and I have to be clean."

He waited.

"Bed, please. Take me to bed. Could you do that? Could you just take me to bed? Could you?"

Afterward he lit cigarettes and called down for ice. He made drinks and took them into the bedroom. She went through hers in a hurry and he built her a second.

She said, "I never exactly told you this, but I'm sort of like a hooker."

"I guessed."

"How? I come on cheap?"

"No amateur could be so skilled."

"I'm serious. How?"

"Well, two and two. Vegas, and this place, and no job or husband. And you said a dancer, and your legs, your muscles are different from a dancer's."

"I didn't think you knew because you never let on. It didn't bother you?"

"Sure it did. It made me impotent."

"Don't joke."

"I'm sorry——"

"No, I'm the one who's sorry, and maybe I need jokes. But didn't you feel anything?"

"Maybe flattered. To be on the free list. You want to tell me about it, Donna?"

"Huh?"

"Because you didn't just wake up tonight and remember the nuns telling you that bad girls go to hell when they die. If you don't want to talk about it, fine, but I get the feeling you do."

"Go to hell. Oh, I didn't mean you, that you should,

I was just being an echo. What you said. Dying and going to hell. Did you ever almost die?"

"Yeah."

"Did you ever have somebody point a gun at you and think you were going to die?"

"Yeah."

"Really? What happened?"

He very nearly said, *I got killed,* but it wasn't the time. "It was in the Army, there were lots of times, but either I shot first or something got me out of it."

"They said he was a banker. Very important, a banker, but he didn't talk like one or act like one. God knows a banker can be as kinky as anybody else, but he was a banker like I'm a boy. He was———"

"Start over."

"What I thought first was he must be like a numbers banker. Or a bookmaker, you know, a major bookmaker that they might call him a banker so he's not just another bookie."

"Start over."

She turned to him. Her eyes worked into focus. "I'm all right now," she told him.

"I know. Want to start over?"

"Okay."

He didn't interrupt. The hysteria had passed and she was able to tell it straight enough now, and he let her do it her way and just lay there on the double bed nursing his drink and taking it all in. The colonel was right, he found himself thinking. You had to draw a line through mankind, a wavy line but a line, and on one side you had Good and on the other side you had Evil. There was good and bad in everyone, sure, and every shitheel was some mother's son, and it was all well and good to know this, but when push came to shove, it was just words; there was Good and Evil with no shades of gray and Judgment Day came seven times a week.

When she ran out of words, Manso stood up. "Stay

right here," he said. "You know where the liquor is. Stay here."

"Eddie, he's got a gun. He'll kill you!"

"Oh, hell," he said. "This is going to kill the image, but all I'm going to do is finish shaving. Because I want to finish shaving, and because I need a few minutes to think about this. Just stay here."

He ran water, spread fresh lather. He was 28, and the face in the mirror looked a little older. This was unusual; for the past three years he had looked 23 almost all the time. But every once in a while his face put on five years. Generally it was heart-shaped and cherubic, topped by a cap of black curls and dimpled on either side of his mouth. Now the planes of his face were harder, and the eyes had turned, and the general impression was no longer one of a moderator of a day-time television show.

He took his time shaving, rinsed, splashed with cold water and after-shave lotion. He thought about beating Platt up, even killing him. Of course there was always the chance that Donna was building fantasies in her head. He could have told her in advance that it was just an act he went through with hookers, say, and Donna later got carried away with the realism of the whole thing.

But what he kept coming back to was this business of Platt insisting he was a banker. A hood who owns banks?

He went back to the bedroom. She was nursing a new drink and smoking another cigarette.

"What bank?"

"Huh?"

"Platt. What's his bank? You said he was talking about it."

"He was a hood, Eddie. Believe me. You live in Vegas and you get to know what a hood is."

"Yeah."

"There are hoods you'll meet who talk like bankers, but I never met a banker who——"

"Yeah. Did he mention the bank?"

"I think so. He said he had three of them."

"Three banks?"

"No, I guess it was two."

"You're sure it wasn't one?"

"No, I'm positive it was two. And he said New Jersey, I remember that much."

"You remember the city?"

"Two cities, one for each bank."

"You remember them?" She didn't. "Hackensack, Jersey City, Newark, Trenton? Camden, uh, New Brunswick, East Orange, uh, Plainfield——"

"I think I'd remember if I heard. Is it important?"

"I don't know. You'd remember if you heard. Jesus, I think I just named every town there is in Jersey. Princeton? Secaucus?"

"No." She thought for a moment. "One of them had *Commerce* in its name."

"That narrows it down."

"I guess it doesn't. You're not . . . you act as though I ought to remember."

"Sorry."

"He was the same way. The one with *Commerce*, that was the one he thought I ought to recognize. He asked me what the hell was wrong with me, didn't I ever listen to a radio? I said yes and he said maybe it wasn't on yet. I don't——"

Eddie was out of bed and on his way to the television set. They watched the last reel of the late show and caught fifteen minutes of news. Nothing. What the hell was Platt talking about?

He fed her drinks until the sun came up, then tucked her in and went downstairs to the casino. There was one crap table open, with three shills trying to feign interest in it. He joined them and felt at least as bored as they were. After half an hour he cashed out a few dollars ahead and had breakfast.

When the New York papers came, he went to work on them. The story was on the first page of the second section of the *Times*. The afternoon before, five masked bandits winged a teller and shot a guard dead and took the Passaic (N.J.) Bank of Commerce and Industry for a sum estimated at slightly in excess of $350,000.

Manso read the brief story twice through, cut it out, read it again, carried it to a phone booth.

"I want to call Tarrytown, New York," he told the operator. "Person-to-person to Colonel Roger Cross." He reached into his pocket, came up with a few quarters and a nickel. "And reverse the charges," he said.

She asked his name and number. "Eddie Manso," he said, and gave the number, which she read back to him. "Make that Corporal Manso," he added. "Corporal Edward J. Manso."

Two

"Extremely interesting," the colonel said. "It might be worthwhile to know just what you've encountered here, Eddie. Now just let me review my thoughts for a moment." His eyes scanned the sheet of notes he had taken during the conversation. His mind caught at ideas, played with them. "Yes," he said at length. "Yes. Extremely interesting. You know, Eddie, we haven't seen you in quite some time. Helen said as much just the other morning. It might be pleasant for all of us if you could arrange a trip east. The day after tomorrow? That's a Thursday, I doubt you'd have any trouble booking a flight. Good, we'll expect you."

The colonel pushed away from his desk, wheeled himself over to the west window. He looked down at the highway and across it to the river below. From that height and distance the Hudson appeared to be as clean and pure as it had been when he had learned to swim in it half a century ago.

But few things seemed as pure after close examination. In April his sister Helen had given him a particularly thoughtful gift on the occasion of his fifty-eighth birthday, a pair of high-quality German binoculars. He enjoyed watching birds through them, but he had learned not to use them when he looked out at the river.

Twenty-five miles to the north on that same river stood West Point, where a sportswriter was the first to name him The Old Rugged Cross. He closed his eyes for a moment and tried to recapture the feeling, playing fullback out of the old single-wing formation, hitting the line hard, blocking for the halfbacks, taking the long snap from center and angling a punt deep for the coffin corner. His right foot ached pleasantly with the memory and he grinned hugely at the brief pain, thinking how utterly the mind and the body live at the mercy of one another.

"What's so funny?"

He turned to smile at his sister. She had a tall drink in her hand and he took it from her. "Time-traveling," he explained. "All of a sudden my foot hurt. It forgot it was somewhere in Laos."

"Do you want a pill? I'll——"

"No, it was just a memory twinge. I was remembering what it was like to kick a football. This"—he raised his glass—"is a superb idea. Aren't you having one?"

"In a little while. Did the phone ring? I was in the yard."

"I took it. It was Eddie Manso."

"Is he in town?"

"No. He's in Las Vegas, as a matter of fact."

"Oh, dear. And he's gambled himself into poverty, I suppose. Shall we wire him a few dollars?"

"Not that at all. He's run into something."

"Oh?"

"Something rather interesting."

Helen's face had clouded briefly when he mentioned his legs, eased when he spoke of Manso. Now as she seated herself in one of the leather chairs she was positively beaming.

"I told Eddie he might come see us on Thursday," he said.

"How marvelous."

"Yes. I might be having the rest of the boys as well. It depends on several things. What time is it?"

"Just past four."

"Do you feel up to some reconnaissance? An hour or so in the library, I should think. You may not get much because I don't know exactly what you would want to look for."

"Just what did Eddie tell you?"

"My notes are on the desk. Bring them over and I'll brief you."

While she was out he stayed in his chair at the window, alternately gazing out over the Hudson and rereading Churchill's *Marlborough*. He had just gotten to the account of the duke's first major victory at Blenheim, and he reviewed Marlborough's strategy and thought how little the basic principles of warfare had changed over the ages. The same general pattern of thrusts and parries worked as well for Marlborough as it had six centuries earlier for William at Hastings. Communications changed, weaponry evolved, armies grew even larger and more complex in structure, but the more things changed, the more they remained as they had always been.

Laos had been the third war for Roger Elliott

Cross. He led a platoon at Salerno and Anzio, fought up and down numbered hills in Korea. When they put together Special Forces, he was one of the first Regular Army types selected, one of the first to see action in Southeast Asia. The men under his command trained tribesmen and villagers, launched hit-and-run missions in Laos and Vietnam.

And he had always liked it. It was hell, as Sherman had said, but at the same time it was a football game for adults, with the sweet harsh joy of contact and the sense of being utterly alive that exists only in the midst of death. Someday, he knew, it would be time to retire. There was the house in Tarrytown, the house he grew up in. There was his sister Helen and her husband Walter. There was enough money to live comfortably on, between the family estate and his own savings and a full colonel's retirement pay. But retirement could wait; he was too busy being alive.

Then one day one of his men took a bullet in the throat just as he pulled the pin of a grenade, and the grenade dribbled across the ground toward Colonel Roger Cross. He woke up in a bed with his legs on fire and when he reached down for them they weren't there. Both gone, one just above the knee, the other halfway up the thigh.

He surprised the hell out of his doctors. They told him he was lucky to be alive, prepared for bitter denial, and he agreed with them completely. He was still the same man as he had been before. A man lived in his mind, and as long as his mind was unimpaired, he remained alive.

He did the exercises. He mended quickly. They flew him from Tokyo to San Francisco to New York, and by the time the jet set down at Kennedy, he was anxious only to see Helen and Walter and make a new life with the two of them. He was confident he would not be a burden. A wheelchair gave one a good deal of mobility and he had learned to use his well. He could amuse himself, he was accustomed to solitude.

Helen met him at the airport, her eyes red from crying. "Now you're being ridiculous," he scolded her. "The important thing is being alive. They say I'm too tough to kill, they broke three hacksaw blades amputating. Pull yourself together, will you? And where in hell is that husband of yours?"

She dissolved completely then, turned and fled from him. He started to wheel the chair in pursuit, then decided to let her be. She came back a few moments later, face washed and hair neat, and told him quickly and concisely what had happened.

Walter was dead. Three weeks ago, while Cross was learning how to operate a wheelchair, Walter Tremont updated his will, paid the delinquent premiums on his insurance policies, and hanged himself in his office.

"I couldn't write you," she said. "I wrote letters, but I couldn't mail them, I had to wait until you were here. When they cut him down his face was all purple and his tongue was huge and black. Oh, Roger——"

A lengthy suicide letter explained everything. Walter Tremont, who had never in his life bet two dollars on a horse race, had lost almost a quarter of a million dollars in Canadian mining stock. He got into it a little at a time, and at first he did well and then he began doing badly, and he plunged deeper and deeper in an effort to get even, and by the time he put the rope around his neck, he had gone through his money and his wife's inheritance and the funds he held in trust for the colonel.

"But he could have gotten back on his feet," Cross said. "He must have known I would have understood. He was a young man, he could have found a way to work things out."

"Roger, he was broken. I . . . the last few weeks I must have made his life miserable. He looked awful, really awful. I kept telling him to see a doctor. I think it would have ruined him physically one way or another even if he hadn't done what he did. Roger, they killed him."

"They?"

The stockbrokers, she told him. Or confidence men, because that was what they really were. A lawyer had gone through Tremont's papers and reconstructed the situation for her. Cross went over it himself and saw that she was right, they had killed him, they had fastened the rope around his neck. It was a boiler room swindle, the main operation based in Toronto with a pair of outside men who had spent months winning Walter Tremont's friendship and setting him up step by step for the kill.

Cross hired detectives. He learned the names of the men who had set up Tremont along with the names of the crew back home in Toronto. He spent time and money assembling folders of evidence, and when he was done, he called in a federal district attorney and showed him what he had.

"He says we haven't got a leg to stand on," he told Helen later. "And then the damned fool blushed like a schoolgirl when he remembered that you're not supposed to use that sort of metaphor in front of a paraplegic. Do schoolgirls still blush? I don't suppose they do. There's no case against those men. They don't seem to have broken any laws. All ten commandments, perhaps, but no laws. God damn it, if I *did* have a leg to stand on, if I had both legs——"

He spent his days reading military theory and history and his nights drinking until sleep came. One day he closed a volume of Clausewitz and shoved the book impatiently aside. Clausewitz didn't tell you how to reach the men who couldn't be reached, the law-abiding thieves who stole a man's money and ruined a man's life.

Or did he? Was it, after all, not a legal problem but a military one, an exercise in strategy and tactics?

He wrote to Washington. He asked the Pentagon for the addresses of men who had served with him in Laos and had since returned to civilian life. The request spent some time going through channels, but eventually he received a list with twenty-three names on it.

He spent two days going over the list and remembering each of the men, assessing strengths and weaknesses, calculating probable motives and desires. At first he planned to get in touch with all of the men, and when he thought about this later on, he guessed that perhaps a dozen of the twenty-three would have responded favorably.

But instead he had picked five men. Four were former enlisted men, only one a commissioned officer. He called those five, and all of them came to Tarrytown, and all of them reacted as he had expected them to react.

And they were good men. It was all the same jungle, he thought, in Laos or the States. It was the same kind of jungle and the same kind of war, and it took the same kind of men to fight it. Men like Manso and Murdock and Simmons and Giordano and Dehn.

Helen returned at six. He asked her if she had found anything, and she said it could wait until after dinner. He argued and she won. He ate a thick slab of roast beef without tasting it. Then, with coffee, she told him what she had learned.

Back in his office he sent four telegrams. To Murdock and Simmons and Giordano and Dehn.

Three

Simmons was mowing the front lawn when the telegram came. He liked to keep the grass just about an inch and a half high, so he had adjusted the blades to that height and mowed the whole lawn, front and back, every Tuesday and Friday evening before dinner. He could have done this at any time of the day, since he worked at home and set his own hours, but he liked to be out there walking behind that big rotary mower when the neighbors drove home from work. Other garden work and home repairs he did when the occasion arose. It was very important, though, that his neighbors could watch him cut that damn grass.

"Howard! Howard!" He cut the mower's engine, walked over to the front door. Esther was framed in the doorway, the light of the setting sun glinting off the lenses of her glasses.

"A telegram," she said.

"Oh, dear Lord," he said.

"I had them read it out to me over the phone."

"Tell me."

"It used to be that they always delivered telegrams in person. Now all it is is a message over the telephone."

He would have liked to shout at her, but this was something he had never done since the day they met. Three years, one child and another coming, and he

23

had never once shouted at her. But it was so maddening the way she fed information in bite-sized pieces, and with the reflected sunlight obscuring her eyes he couldn't read her face.

He approached her, took her arm. "Bad news?"

"Well, no. But bad for me. I wrote it down." She turned and he followed her into the house. "Another collection coming on the market, so I suppose that's another business trip. Here."

The message read: OPPORTUNITY NEGOTIATE PUR-CHASE HIGH TICKET EUROPEAN COLLECTION STRONG NINETEENTH CENTURY CLASSICS RECOMMEND THURS-DAY ARRIVAL. It was signed ROGER CROSS.

"I suppose you're going?"

"If you like food on the table, then I'm going."

"I like food on the table. I like my husband home, too. Where is it you're going?"

"Cross is in New York," he said. "I'll have to meet him there, but most likely the collection will be somewhere halfway across the country, and I'll be chasing after it."

"Why aren't there ever any collections here in Detroit? You'd think there wasn't a stamp collector in the entire state of Michigan, but I just suppose when they think on selling they call in some dealer from Arizona or New Mexico. Didn't this Roger Cross send you a telegram before?"

He nodded. "Sort of a vest-pocket dealer. He'll run into things like this that aren't in his line, you see, and if I make a deal I'll pay him a commission."

"I just hope you won't be gone long as last time. Two months and you're going to be a daddy again, you know. Be nice if you were around for it."

He came up behind her, put his arms around her, clasped his hands over her abdomen. "Nice little baby," he said.

"Oh, now."

His hands moved upward to her large breasts. "Lucky baby. What nice lunch bags, I declare."

She giggled, delighted, then shook herself free. "How you carry on, Howard Simmons. Now I've got dinner to fix, and you have a lawn to mow. You don't want them saying you don't keep up your property, do you?"

"And aren't those my property, Queen Esther?"

"Go on, now," she said.

After dinner he called Northwest Orient and made a reservation for Wednesday night. He bathed little Martin and played with him until bedtime, then sat with Esther in front of the color television set. He couldn't keep his mind on the programs, and after a while he didn't even try. He thought about the telegram from the colonel and wondered what it would turn out to be.

He found himself wondering if the men liked him. The colonel did, he knew, but sometimes he felt a little ill at ease with the other men, as if his presence made them indefinably uncomfortable. He knew he was inclined to be overly sensitive, it was the way he was, and of course you couldn't get away from the class division even in civilian life. He had been an officer, a captain, and they were enlisted men, and that in its own way created a gulf at least as great as the other element that separated him from them.

The first time, in Canada, he had been particularly aware of the distance between himself and Dehn and Giordano and Murdock and Manso. More with Murdock than the others, perhaps, but it was there with all of them. Still, he had to admit that it had never gotten in the way. The five of them worked together on an equal level, planned the operation and carried it through, and when they were all together with the colonel in the big house in Tarrytown, the pie was carved into equal shares, a shade over fifty thousand in cash money for each of them.

"I want to thank you all," the colonel had said. "You'll all go back to your own separate lives now. I don't suppose we'll see each other much, if at all. But if any of you ever needs anything, anything at all——"

Then a sort of embarrassed pause, until Giordano said what all of them had been thinking. "Sir, I'll say one thing. This past month makes the first time I've felt like myself since I took off that uniform, sir."

Nods and echoes. And Ben Murdock, elaborately casual, saying, "You know, this kind of thing, we could do it again sometime."

The six of them were up all night talking about it. All over the country there were dirty men with dirty money, men the law could never get close to, but once you took their money away, it turned clean. Hard, tough men—but after fun and games in Laos you weren't so easily impressed by tough men in civvies. As the colonel said, it was all the same jungle, and jungle fighting was what they were trained for.

The colonel helped plan out their lives for them. They needed covers, he told them. They needed lives that would account for their income, needed ways to bury their money and turn dirty money into clean money.

For Simmons, the answer was a simple one. All his life, ever since his second-grade teacher gave him some stamps from letters from her mother in Hungary, he had spent spare time working on his stamp collection. It wasn't much of a collection because he had never earned huge money, but it was perfectly organized and beautifully mounted. And ever since he decided against reenlisting and went back to Detroit and found Esther and married her, ever since then he'd had that one big dream. Sooner or later, damn it, he was going to be a stamp dealer.

An independent dealer. No shop, no boss, no customers to meet face to face, even. Ads in the magazines and all his business done by mail, and Lord, if he only had the capital, he could do it right. None of the penny-ante stuff, no fooling with new issues and other promotional items. Just buying and selling good solid collectible stamps.

It was the perfect cover. The fifty thousand from Operation Stockpile was enough to buy the house and the stamp stock and keep the business running a long time. As it turned out, the business went into the black by the fourth month; last year he had netted better than twelve thousand dollars just selling stamps. And the two operations they had carried out since then were gravy. It was a cinch to hide the proceeds, paying cash for expensive stamps for his own collection. His personal collection was quite an improvement on that handful of Hungarian stamps that started him off twenty-seven years ago. He wondered what Esther would say if she knew how much it was worth.

And later, in bed, after he had successfully convinced her that lovemaking would not constitute an invasion of the baby-to-be's privacy, he listened to her measured breathing and wished he didn't have to keep this part of his life secret from her. It was for her own good, he knew. She worried enough if he got on a plane, and if she had the slightest idea what he really did on those business trips, it would tear her up, no question about it.

Still, though, there were times when he ached to tell her, if only for the fun of checking out her reaction. He decided that she just wouldn't believe it, any more than his mail-order stamp customers would believe that Howard Simmons was a Negro.

Four

It was clear hot weather in Joplin, so Dehn took the day off. He generally took off three or four days a week, not counting Saturdays and Sundays. If the weather was good, he liked to spend his time on a golf course. If it wasn't, he sure as hell didn't want to go around ringing doorbells. But once or twice a week the weather would be sufficiently unremarkable as to make golf unappealing and doorbell-ringing bearable, and on those days he would walk the streets of whatever city he happened to be in and try to sell some poor clown an encyclopedia.

He was pretty good at it because he got such a kick out of people. He traveled for a good encyclopedia, one of the two or three best, and he didn't feel at all dishonest about conning people into buying it. When you came right down to it, nobody really needed an encyclopedia. A staggering number of people lived full and rewarding lives without ever being in the same house with an encyclopedia. On the other hand, though, if a guy was going to waste his money on something, he could do a lot worse. It certainly didn't hurt you to have an encyclopedia in the house. It wasn't like selling liquor or cigarettes or automobiles. Nobody ever got killed by an encyclopedia.

Because he got a kick out of people, and because he regarded both his work and his customers with the ideal mixture of sincerity and contempt, Dehn was a pretty decent salesman. He averaged close to a sale a week, and with his net on a sale pegged at $168.50 he earned not too much less money than he spent. He had figured that he ought to pay taxes on around ten thou a year. He made up the difference now and then by sending in an order and paying for it himself, generally with a money order drawn under a fictitious name. He had the sets delivered to orphanages and old folks' homes as anonymous gifts, with the commissions that came back to him from the Chicago office boosting his income to a sufficiently realistic figure.

That day he got out to the golf course early. He hung around the clubhouse until three other loners accumulated, then played eighteen holes with them as a foursome. He hooked most of his tee shots, but his short game was on and he came in with an 82, which was a little better than he averaged on that course.

The weather was just as good that afternoon. He was going to play around again after lunch but changed his mind and put his clubs in the trunk. He drove out Grand Avenue into one of the newer developments and went around punching doorbells. The first fifteen houses he didn't even get a foot in the door. The sixteenth was a bottle-blond housewife with her kids in school and her husband at the plant, and after two and a half hours in her bedroom he' could have sold her six encyclopedias and a second-hand Edsel, but he didn't even try. He had done that once and it made him feel too much like a pimp.

He drove back to his motel and read *Hydroz* to *Jerem* until it was time to go out for dinner. He ate downtown, caught a movie, stopped at a drugstore for an ice cream soda, and got back to the motel around nine thirty. The telegram was waiting at the desk for him.

Dehn generally worked a new town for three or four weeks, and whenever he moved, he sent the colonel his address. He had mailed a great many postcards to Tarrytown since the last operation. Now, as the clerk passed him the telegram, his heart pounded faster.

In his room he read: REGRET TO INFORM YOU AUNT HARRIET DIED PEACEFULLY IN HER SLEEP LAST NIGHT FUNERAL THURSDAY. ROGER.

He left the telegram on the nightstand. It took him twenty minutes to pack his suitcases and settle his bill. Another ten minutes and he was on 66 heading east. "Poor Aunt Hattie," he said. "I wonder if she mentioned me in her will."

Five

When Giordano opened his travel agency in Phoenix, a few of his friends told him he ought to change his name. "Because face it, Lou," one of them said, "there's this image people have of Italians. Me, I'm in construction, an Italian builder is something the average Joe can understand. But who's gonna do business with a travel agent named Giordano?"

"Anybody who wants to go to Rome," Giordano said.

Not many people did, as it happened. Giordano's Travel Bureau occupied three magnificently appointed rooms in the best office building in downtown Phoenix, and Giordano himself occupied a penthouse at the Wentworth Arms, and everyone knew he had to be grossing better than fifty thousand a year. Everybody was wrong. The travel agency had everything but customers, largely because Giordano spent so much of his time traveling on his own and so little time handling business. He made enough to cover the salaries of the two girls who worked for him. His books—the ones he consulted when he filed his tax return—showed a net profit for the past year of twenty-one thousand dollars. The real books showed a slight loss, but not enough of one to get concerned about.

Giordano was 31, toothpick thin, with straight brown hair and angular features. He went into the Army looking like the 97-pound weakling in the Charles Atlas ads, and he enlisted in the hope that the service would build him up. He did put on a few pounds at first, and the little flesh he carried on his frame turned almost at once to muscle, but he never did stop looking undernourished. By the time he came home from Laos, a bad dose of malaria had him looking as bad as he did when he enlisted, and a hell of a lot older. On top of everything else, somewhere in the course of things his eyesight deteriorated, so now he was not only a shrimp but a shrimp who wore glasses.

He fooled people. Thin frame, thin legs, wrists like a schoolgirl, thick glasses, he fooled people all the time. When the colonel got them all together in Philadelphia for Operation Sharkbait, he planted himself as an invalid accountant with a ton of hospital bills. He got into the loan shark for a couple of thousand, not because the money mattered—the big score was almost forty times that figure—but in order to get a closer look at the loan shark's operation.

The timing got slightly screwed up on that operatin. The shark sent a couple of muscle boys after Giordano before the squad was ready to pull the chain, and Giordano came home one day to find a pair of heavies waiting in his room. He played his part as long as he could, whining and begging and promising to pay, but scaring wasn't enough. They had orders to rough him up a little. His better judgment told him to take the beating, that they were pros and wouldn't overdo it, but when they reached for him, his reflexes took over. He flipped one of the goons off a wall and chopped the other one in the Adam's apple. Then he stood looking down at them and cursed himself quietly for jeopardizing the whole score. If they went back to their boss with the news that the sick, puny accountant was a tiger in disguise, things could suddenly get very sticky.

So he gave them each an extra chop in the neck. After he had made sure that they were both properly dead, he made a phone call, and Murdock and Frank Dehn drove over in a truck and carried the two hoods out in a pair of steamer trunks. They shipped them both express collect to Seattle. Giordano checked the papers for weeks afterward and never saw a line about it.

Giordano fooled women, too. They started off feeling sorry for him, certain they would be safe with him. The outcome surprised them as much as it surprised the two hoods in Philadelphia, although the women rarely felt bad about it. He used a sort of mental karate, pitching the charm at just the right level until they felt that they could perform the kindest and most charitable act of their lives by going to bed with him. The next thing they knew they were hysterical with passion. By morning they would be madly in love with Giordano, who would never see them again. It wasn't a matter of principle with him. He had told friends that he was spending his entire life looking for a woman he would want to see a second time, and he just hadn't found her yet.

Nor did he intend to abandon the search. On Tuesday night his telephone rang while he was searching industriously with a six-foot Swedish blonde whose breasts each weighed about as much as Giordano. The phone picked a very bad time to ring, and Giordano flipped the receiver onto the floor and went back to what he was doing. He never did get around to putting it back on the hook, so he didn't get the colonel's wire until he went to the office the next morning.

"Get me on an afternoon flight to Kennedy," he told one of his girls. "Round-trip, return open. Call United first, but check the movie for me before you make it firm. Then call the Plaza in New York or, if they're full, the Pierre. Tell them just overnight."

He didn't have to worry about packing. He had a bag packed and ready in his office. There were two suits in it, plus shirts and socks and underwear and a full complement of toilet articles. There was also a pair of throwing knives, a strip of very thin, very strong steel, and a small-caliber automatic pistol.

The girl looked up from the phone. "Oh, Lou," she said, "was that first-class or tourist? I don't think you said."

"Oh, make it first-class," he told her. "They give us a discount."

Six

By the time Murdock got back to his rooming house Tuesday night, he couldn't have told a telegram from a turbojet. He was in Minneapolis working on and off for a firm of short-haul movers, and he had spent most of that day moving a family from a third-floor apartment on Horatio to a fourth-floor apartment just three blocks away on Van Duyzen. One stairwell was worse than the other, and they had a baby grand piano that was a bitch on wheels. By the time he was through, a beer sounded like one fine idea. After a half dozen bottles of Hamm's it seemed like an even better idea to switch to something a mite more powerful. He woke up with vague memories of a fight in one place and of dragging ass when the owner called the cops, and then going over to some other place that some good old boy knew about and starting in all over again. Somewhere along the line he evidently decided to pack it in and head for home, and damned if he hadn't found his way, but he couldn't remember that part of it at all.

He threw his legs over the side of the bed and sat up. He tried to remember if he had told the boss he would be coming to work that day. It didn't make such a much whether he did or not, because fish would fly before he'd show up at that moving company, but if they were expecting him, it meant he'd be out a job. Or maybe he wouldn't; most of the moving companies took what they could get and didn't expect you to be reliable. Which was good news, because if there was one thing Ben Murdock wasn't, reliable is what it was.

He was just created to raise hell, a lanky redneck with hair like straw and a mean streak that just had to pop out now and again. If he stood in the sun, freckles popped out on his face and forearms, and if he stood anywhere for any length of time, sun or shade, the meanness popped out the same way and he was ace-high certain to buy trouble for himself. He grew up in Tennessee and got thrown out of school over and over again, and when he was nineteen, he had to take off and drive up to Chicago because of a difference of opinion with a girl. His opinion was that she was sort of in the mood no matter what she said, and her opinion was that he had raped her. When she made her opinion known to the police, he borrowed himself a car and pointed it north.

They never did get him for the car he borrowed, but within a month they picked him up for drinking after hours. He did the drinking in the middle of State Street and he got the liquor by putting his foot through the store window. The judge gave him a suspended sentence.

He was in jail twice, Cook County Jail, ten days and then twenty, both times for drunk and disorderly. A little bit after he got out, he borrowed another car and cracked it up, and another judge gave him a choice between the Army and Joliet. He took the Army because he figured it would be a sight easier to bust out of.

He stayed in for fifteen years. They tried to bust his ass in basic and they just couldn't do it, but while they were working on it something happened and they made a good soldier out of him. He made squad leader, he made Expert Rifleman. Somebody told him that they gave you double pay in the Paratroops, and he told him to shove it because all the money in the world wouldn't get him to jump out of a plane. Then one of his bunkmates said that the Paratroops were the toughest outfit in the service, and that all they got lately was colored boys because no white man would stand up to it. He thought about that for a day and night, and the morning after that he went in and volunteered for the Paratroops.

He went Special Forces first time it was offered. He made corporal eight times and was busted back down eight times, but he never did anything bad enough to earn him a discharge or a stretch of stockade time. Just something about that old Army, he fit and he belonged and it was more a home to him than Tennessee ever was and not to say Chicago. He reckoned they would kill him sooner or later, but he also reckoned he'd stay with it until they did.

Until one day on a patrol when he made the mistake of getting in a sniper's sights and the sniper made the mistake of putting two hunks of lead in Murdock's left arm and missing the rest of him altogether. After they patched him up, he asked when he could rejoin his unit. They told him he had a million-dollar wound, a pin in his shoulder and another pin in his elbow, and that was the last he and the Army would be seeing of each other.

They told him he was a hero and he'd get a pension and he should be happy. He wasn't happy. He couldn't figure why the sniper couldn't either do the job right or miss him altogether, because now he was just sure to go on back and buy himself some trouble. Just a couple of pissant steel pins that he never so much as knew were there unless it was raining, and for that they took him and chucked him out of his home after fifteen years.

He got up from the bed, went over to the washbowl, and rinsed some of the sour taste out of his mouth. When he turned to reach for a towel, he saw the telegram lying alongside the door. He knew what it was right away. He opened it and it was the usual message: COME HOME AT ONCE YOUR MOTHER IS DEAD. PA. The colonel didn't like sending that message, but Murdock insisted on it. If there was one person on earth he purely hated, it was his mother. It surely tickled him to get that telegram.

He looked in his pants pockets. He had a five-dollar bill left and a couple of ones, and there was a handful of change on the dresser. He got his knife and pried up the linoleum in one corner of the room. His travel money was still there, five hundred-dollar bills and two tens. That was one thing he never touched was his travel money, no matter how drunk he got or how broke he was. Not unless the colonel sent him that wire, which was what that particular money was reserved for.

He went across the hall to the bathroom, took himself a shower, went back to his room, and put on his best clothes. He polished his good shoes with the bath towel.

He left everything else in the room. The landlady could keep them or throw them out, her choice. He could care less. He was going back to where he belonged, with the good old boys who liked to move out and all the same as he did. Old Rugged Cross with his legs gone, and Eddie and Frank and the skinny dago and the nigger captain, and by God he was going to have himself some fun.

Seven

The colonel waited patiently while Helen Tremont wheeled the tea cart around the oval oak table, serving mugs of coffee and wedges of Danish pastry to each of the five men. When she left the room, he leaned forward, his arms on the table before him.

He said, "Albert Platt. Born September four, nineteen twenty-one in Brooklyn. Raised in the Brownsville and East New York sections of that borough. Arrested nineteen thirty-six for auto theft, served six months in Chatworth Reformatory. Nineteen thirty-eight to forty-one, arrested five times on charges ranging from simple assault to rape. Charges dropped for lack of evidence. Inducted into the armed forces in nineteen forty-two, dishonorably discharged later that same year. Arrested nineteen forty-four, assault with a deadly weapon. Charges dropped. Arrested nineteen forty-six, homicide. Witnesses refused to testify. Arrested nineteen forty-eight, homicide. Witness mysteriously disappeared, charges dropped."

The colonel sipped at his coffee. "No arrests since nineteen forty-eight," he said. "Until that date Platt operated primarily in Brooklyn and Long Island. In nineteen forty-eight he moved across the river to New Jersey. He established a connection with a group of New Jersey racketeers, including Philip Longostini, known to intimates as Phil the Lobster. Longostini's interests included several restaurants and nightclubs in Bergen County, two suburban garbage collection services, a vending machine corporation, two bowling alleys, and a chain of laundry and dry-cleaning establishments. He was also reputed to control bookmaking and loan shark operations in northern New Jersey, and wielded unofficial power in at least three labor unions.

"By nineteen fifty-two Platt had established himself as Longostini's chief enforcer—I believe that's the term?" He looked for confirmation to Manso, who nodded. "Platt's activities in this capacity were not such as to lead to his arrest, but it would seem that at least a dozen acts of murder were carried out either by him or under his orders." The colonel placed the tips of his fingers together and looked thoughtfully at them. "I have read that one should be pleased when criminals turn to legitimate enterprise, that this will in some mysterious way effect their reform. This is a witless notion. The only result is that the enterprise itself becomes illegitimate. For that matter, I have read that crime does not pay and that criminals come to a bad end. Philip Longostini's bad end came in July of nineteen sixty-four at his four-acre estate in Englewood Cliffs. He died peacefully in his sleep at the age of seventy-three and left an estate estimated at . . . well, this is immaterial, isn't it?"

The colonel's eyes worked their way around the table, focusing in turn upon Murdock and Dehn and Simmons and Giordano and Manso. He said, "Edward?"

"Sir?"

"The photographs."

Manso passed him a large Manila envelope. The colonel opened the clasp and withdrew half a dozen 8-by-11 photos. "Edward was able to take these in Las

Vegas," he said. "Albert Platt appears in each. In this photograph you will note the man immediately on Platt's right. Edward?"

"Buddy Rice. He drives Platt's car and bodyguards him."

"I believe you said he carries a gun."

Manso nodded. "A forty-five in a shoulder rig. He's also supposed to be very good with a knife."

Dehn said, "You got all this in Vegas?"

"I spent a day asking a few questions."

"He get any kind of a make on you?"

"I don't think so. We were at the same crap table once, but between the broad on his arm and the trouble the dice were giving him I don't think he paid any attention to me."

The colonel waited until the photos made their way around the table and returned to him. He gathered them up and put them back in the envelope. He drank more coffee, set the cup down empty. "So much for the background," he said. "You'll want to take detailed notes from here on in." He waited while the five uncapped pens and opened pocket notebooks. "Platt did not take over all of Longostini's operations," he began. "You'll understand that the newspapers were vague on this, but my sister has become rather adept at research. She went beyond the usual coverage and pieced out details from the accounts of several senatorial investigations. Platt seems to be in direct control of approximately a third of organized criminal activity in Bergen County and the surrounding area. His income from legitimate sources alone is quite high. He lives in a pre-Revolutionary estate on four acres of land just south of Tenafly. The grounds are walled off and patrolled by armed guards. Rumors circulate that associates of his who have disappeared over the years are buried in wooded areas of the estate.

"But that, too, is largely immaterial. More to the point, Platt has broadened and extended the scope of his operations. As I said, he did not take over completely upon Longostini's death. He gave up gambling interests in return for full control of loan shark activities. And, early in nineteen sixty-six, he widened his interests to include the banking business. It was at that time that he acquired control of the Passaic Bank of Commerce and Industry."

Simmons said, "With a criminal record?"

"His control is unofficial. The president of the bank is Jerome Gegner, who has no criminal record. Gegner's former employment includes a stint as manager of the Thirty-Thirty Club in Paterson. He also served as vice-president and treasurer of Harco Automatic Vending, Inc. Both of these firms were originally owned by Philip Longostini. Members of the board of directors of the Passaic Bank of Commerce and Industry include several other known associates of Platt's. One of them is surprisingly young to be a bank director. His name is Silvertree. Oddly enough, he happens to be married to Albert Platt's niece."

The colonel paused to give the note-takers a chance to catch up. Some of them, he knew, would be able to read back his words almost verbatim. Dehn and Simmons were like this. Murdock, on the other hand, would write down almost nothing, preferring to rely on his memory.

"Banking and finance seems an odd choice for Platt," he said at length. "When Eddie brought this whole matter up, my first reaction was that Platt must be the organizer or financier of a gang of robbers. The idea of criminal interests actually owning a bank did not even occur to me. Since then I've learned more about criminal resourcefulness. It seems Platt was only following a current trend in gangster circles. As long ago as nineteen sixty, men like Platt have sought out banks with a rather poor profit picture, banks that may be acquired with little difficulty. There are several banks in the Chicago area that are known to be under mob control, along with one on Long Island and several others in various parts of the country.

"They serve a very valuable function. For one thing, they provide an ideal cover for the extraordinary cash flow involved in criminal enterprises. They also permit loan sharks to cloak themselves in an aura of legitimacy. Suppose, for example, that a businessman wants to borrow a truly substantial sum of money. A hundred thousand dollars, let us say. His credit situation is such that he cannot obtain the loan from a legitimate source. He goes to Platt, who loans him the money at standard terms, except that the borrower signs a note, not for the hundred thousand he receives, but for twice that amount. Thus Platt has a bona fide note for two hundred thousand dollars, along with a staff of thugs to make sure that the debt is eventually collected. And his books show no profit beyond the legal interest on the principal of the note; the extra hundred thousand dollars is invisible profit.

"That's just one example. There could be any number of others. A man in Platt's position inevitably handles large sums of hot money that have to be rechanneled into circulation. A bank serves admirably in this respect. No doubt he functions as a broker for other criminals as well. You remember the Ackermann kidnapping, of course. The details slip my mind, but as I recall there was a quarter of a million dollars worth of marked bills involved, and none of that money has yet turned up in circulation. A crook with a bank at his disposal could purchase that ransom money from the kidnappers for thirty or forty cents on the dollar and simply hold it as cash reserves until the heat died down."

Giordano asked if there was any connection between Platt and the Ackermann kidnapping. The colonel said there was not. "Just what use Platt has made of his banks is immaterial," he said.

Dehn said, "Banks?"

"Yes. He acquired a second just a little over a year ago. The Commercial Bank of New Cornwall, also in Bergen County. You'll want to write that down. No, we don't know just what use Platt has made of these banks, except that he seems to have been an innovator in one respect. He's found an original way to increase his banks' profit."

"How?"

"By robbing them."

Giordano had to admit it was brilliant. He listened carefully as the colonel went through the whole thing, and his own mind began racing on ahead, playing with the possibilities of the whole thing. He had thought he knew of most of the standard gambits. Fire insurance, for example. There were an incredible number of ways to burn down one's property for the insurance, and he knew of so many cases that he often wondered if a fire had ever started by accident. From what he knew, you could make out fairly nicely that way. If you had a business that was losing money, you just made sure you were carrying the right type and amount of insurance, and then you crossed two wires and went home. That way you wound up with a little more than the business was conceivably worth, and you avoided the headache of finding somebody who was fool enough to buy it.

It was a great way out of a bad situation, he thought, but not much more than that; there was no way to have both the business and the money. This bank dodge, though—that was something else entirely.

You started out by setting it up right, finding some excuse to have the maximum amount of cash in the vault. Then you sent your own men in, and they had less trouble knocking the place over than you'd have opening a can of peas. They made it look good, maybe even tossed a few bullets around for added realism. You, in turn, made sure somebody went through the motions of turning in the alarm—but not so quick as to create any hassles. The federal investigators came in and they investigated, and all they found out was that the bank had been robbed. The Federal Deposit Insurance Corporation made most of the loss good, and whatever they didn't cover would show on the bank's books as a loss and would just save you that much more in taxes. So you wound up with the cash you had robbed, plus the cash from the FDIC, plus the loss on the books. And if any of the money from the bank happened to be hot, you just put it back in the vault and let it sit on ice until it cooled off again.

When the colonel finished, Giordano lifted his hand. "It's very neat, sir," he said. "But one thing. It's sort of one-time-only, isn't it? Platt can do this once and score for whatever it was, three hundred fifty thou, but he can't do it again, can he?"

"No."

"Because the feds would have a tip to it. Even now they might have a good idea of what happened, but unless they find the robbers and tie them to Platt, they can't do a thing about it. But if he tried it again, they could put him in a box."

"That's correct."

Simmons said, "Of course he has two banks. He might try the same trick with the other bank."

"Maybe in ten years," Giordano said. "Not before then."

"Because they would make a connection, Louis?"

"They'd have to, sir. This Platt, I would guess he's hoping nobody else just happens to knock off one of his banks. Because if either one of them gets hit, a lot of people are going to take a long look at Mr. Platt."

He studied the colonel. There was the ghost of a smile on the colonel's lips, and Giordano got it. "Oh," he said. "Oh."

The colonel said, "Operation Bankroll."

Giordano was nodding to himself. He looked around the table, one face after another, and now they all got it.

"Operation Bankroll," the colonel repeated. "The Commercial Bank of New Cornwall. That's Mr. Platt's bank, gentlemen, and we are going to roll right over it."

Eight

The pickup truck was blue, with STEDMAN'S TREE SURGERY / LAMBERTVILLE, PA. lettered in white on the sides. The back of the truck held a couple of saws, a bucket of creosote, a stepladder, and a mound of branches and odd cuttings. Simmons, dressed in overalls and a denim cap, sat behind the wheel. Murdock was at the side door of the house talking to the woman.

"See, my helper, he noticed it from the road," Murdock was saying. "Tell the truth, I wouldn't of seen it myself, but then he's got sharp eyes for a nigger."

"A Negro," the woman said.

"Yes, ma'am. Anyway, he seen it and slowed down, and I took a look, and that limb's got to come off, ma'am. The borers is into it so bad there's no saving it. The rest of the tree is sound, they'll do like that sometimes, but that one limb is rotten with borers, and all they can do is spread. I ain't saying she's got to come off this minute or the tree'll be gone tomorrow, nothing like that. But I will say that they'll be on into the trunk by fall and be killing that tree by next spring."

The woman said, "Termites."

"No, borers is what they are. Termites you'll get in houses, in dead wood, but borers——"

"We had a man who insisted the house was crawling with termites. He offered to clear them out for three

44

hundred dollars." The woman smiled frigidly. "We found out it was a racket."

Murdock had his cap in his hands. He was twisting it, and Simmons fought back a laugh. Thick-soled boots and blue jeans and that flannel shirt and twisting his cap—the perfect redneck, Simmons thought.

"Well, Miz Tuthill," Murdock said. "Well, now. Termite inspectors, well you don't have to tell me about them."

"He said he was just passing through," Mrs. Tuthill said. "And for that reason he would do the job at a special rate. We didn't even have any termites, as it happened."

"Well," Murdock said. "Well, borers you sure do have, Miz Tuthill. You come and look at that tree and you'll see them borers. Why, from where you're standing you can see how the leaves is growing funny. You see that big red oak there? See where I'm pointing? Now can you see the second branch from the bottom on the right? See those leaves, how they're a sort of a paler shade of green, kind of on the sick side?"

The woman was nodding.

"Now I'll tell you true, Miz Tuthill, ma'am, not like any old termite inspector. We don't entirely wait for work to come our way. You can't, not in this business. Mr. Stedman, what he says——"

"Oh, then you're not Mr. Stedman?"

"No, ma'am." Murdock smiled. "Why, there's better than twenty of us works for Mr. Stedman, he's the biggest tree surgeon in all eastern Pennsylvania. What he says, he says you have to look for work that has to be done. He says by the time the average person notices something wrong with a tree, why, it's too late to do more than cut the whole thing down. An oak like that, an oak that must of took forty, fifty years to grow, it's a powerful shame to lose it."

"Well," Mrs. Tuthill said. "Perhaps if my husband agrees, I could call your Mr. Stedman tomorrow and——"

"Ma'am, if you was to call Mr. Stedman, we'd be glad to come, but that limb, the sawing of it isn't but a ten-dollar piece of work, and for us to come all the way clear up from Lambertville——"

"Oh, my. Only ten dollars?"

"What with us being here now, ma'am, she wouldn't be any more than that. Oh, I see, you was recollecting that termite inspector and three hundred dollars. Now if you wanted to call the Better Business Bureau in Lambertville, or if——"

"Oh, for heaven's sake." Mrs. Tuthill was laughing now. "Oh, my, ten dollars, and here I thought . . . oh, for heaven's sake, cut the silly thing off. Ten dollars!"

"It seems wrong," Simmons said. "Cutting a perfectly good limb off a perfectly good tree."

"Shucks," Murdock said, "I reckon it would have had borers sooner or later."

"Telling her to look how the leaves are growing." The road swung around to the left, and Simmons tapped the brake pedal lightly. The truck rolled into the curve. "That lawn, now, that's something else. You see how patchy it was? That comes from cutting it too low, that and using the wrong seed mix."

"Soon as we're all set up, you can go back and do Mrs. Tuthill's lawn for her."

"Somebody should. Those burnt-out patches, that comes from using a fertilizer with too much phosphate. Of course, now, to do the right kind of work on a lawn that size——"

"You suppose it'd cost as much as cleaning out her termites?"

Simmons laughed.

"Does seem like a waste," Murdock went on. "Climbing her damn tree and sawing the damn limb off and daubing on the creosote and all just for a reference. And you damn well know Platt ain't going to call her anyway."

"Colonel Cross says he might."

"Platt? Gangster like him, that kind of a bad old boy, nice old lady like Mrs. Tuthill wouldn't give him the time of day."

Simmons shrugged. "Might try to call Mr. Stedman in Lambertville. Might have some trouble, since there's no Mr. Stedman in Lambertville——"

"There really a Lambertville?"

"Must be. Colonel says we need a reference. Colonel has a habit of being right. That's Platt's place on the right."

"And who says crime don't pay?"

Simmons braked the truck and slowed to a crawl. While Murdock checked out the trees on the front lawn, Simmons clicked off mental pictures of the estate itself. Eighty yards of frontage rimmed by a ten-foot iron fence. A gate in the center opening onto a circular driveway. The main house, huge, white, fronted by massive columns. A garage off to the left, with living quarters over it. The grounds, Simmons noted, were very well kept.

He said, "He just might already have a tree surgeon, Ben."

"He's got a tree that's dying."

"Really?"

Murdock pointed at an aged silver maple. "Storm damage. See where the lightning caught it? Wonder what the hell you'd do with something like that."

"You're the doctor."

Murdock grinned. Simmons pulled to a stop at the gate. Guards stood on either side, thick-bodied men wearing revolvers on their hips. The one on Murdock's side also carried a carbine.

Murdock drawled, "Stedman's Tree Surgery, here to see Mr. Platt."

The guard with the carbine shook his head.

"Not home?"

"No."

Murdock grinned easily. "Think my boy and I'll just have a look at that tree if we might." He started to open the door. The guard leaned on it and Murdock let it swing shut.

The guard said, "Nobody comes on the grounds without Mr. Platt says it's okay."

Murdock hesitated, then heaved a sigh. "Well," he said. "I'll just phone him up tonight."

"You do that," the guard said.

Back on the road Murdock said, "Seemed worth a try."

"I didn't think they'd go for it."

"Not the way those two take to playing soldier. Two guards, two of them, and that fat one can't make do with just a revolver, he needs a bee-bee gun, too. You catch the fancy belt and holster?"

"That's hand-tooled leather."

"Nothing but the finest. Reckon they can shoot worth spit?"

"I have a feeling they practice a lot."

"I guess," Murdock said. He took a cigarette and gave one to Simmons. They smoked for a while in silence. "I'll call him tonight, we'll do the job in the morning. Lawn looked good, didn't it?"

"Like a golf course."

"Means he probably thought about getting a tree doctor in and never got around to it. We'll make it all good tomorrow. How'd you like that fat boy on the gate, anyhow?"

"They were both fat."

"Yeah. I sure had a longing to take the two of them."

"So did I," Simmons said.

Nine

The Commercial Bank of New Cornwall was located at the northwest corner of the intersection of Broad Street and Revere Avenue. Broad Street was the main commercial thoroughfare of the town, and the one-story brick building fronted on Broad with a small parking lot alongside on Revere. Dehn put his car in the lot and walked around to the front entrance. It was fifteen minutes past three. The bank normally closed at three, but on Fridays it stayed open until 5:30.

Dehn opened the door, went inside. He was wearing a gray sharkskin suit and carrying a slim leather attaché case. His glance darted around the bank, registering impressions, estimating distances. He wouldn't have to supply details. Giordano, who had visited the bank during the noon rush, would probably be able to come up with a virtual floor plan of the layout. But Dehn wanted to get his own feel of the place, and it wouldn't hurt for him to be able to backstop Giordano.

A row of tellers' cages on the right. A stand-up desk in the center where depositors could fill out slips. On the left, three desks for bank officers, just one of them presently occupied. A staircase at the rear center, presumably leading to the vault room in the basement. A uniformed guard at the head of the stairs, another at the side door, plus the one he had passed in front. The guards themselves looked wholly interchangeable, stiff

49

white-haired men with slight paunches and underslung jaws. Dehn guess they were retired cops.

Dehn went over to the desk where a bank officer sat. When the man looked up from a column of figures, he said he wanted to open a checking account. The officer pointed him to a chair, opened a desk drawer, asked if he was interested in a regular or a special checking account, He started to explain the difference, and Dehn cut in and said the regular account would be fine. The officer brightened at this.

Dehn gave his name as Arthur Moorehead of Seattle, explained he had taken a position in New Cornwall and would be bringing his family east as soon as he found suitable accommodations for them. "But first you set the financial house in order," the banker said. "Good, good."

A year earlier Dehn had opened an account as Arthur Moorehead at the Shippers' Bank of Seattle. He had closed out the account within a week, but somehow or other he had never destroyed the checkbook. He wrote out a check now for $2,500 and used it to open his account.

The bank official said something tentative about waiting a week for imprinted checks.

"Oh, of course," Dehn said. "You'll want to wait until my check clears Seattle. No problem. I won't need to draw on this account for the time being."

It would take the check at least ten days to bounce back to New Cornwall. And by that time the bank would have more important things to worry about than Arthur Moorehead.

After the last of the forms had been filled out, Dehn asked about a safe deposit box. They only had a small selection, he was told, and there was a waiting list for the larger boxes, but a small one might be available. Was that satisfactory?

Dehn said it was. The officer went away, came back, smiled, and led him down the stairs at the rear. There was a massive gate at the foot of the stairs, with an

electric eye beam between the stairs and the gate. A
guard came into view when they broke the beam. He
and the bank officer nodded to each other, and the
guard pressed a button to release an electronic lock.
Inside was the bank's own vault and, to the left, a few
dozen feet of wall space given over to individual safe
deposit boxes.

In a curtained booth Dehn opened the box and took
from his attaché case a thick manila envelope sealed
with heavy plastic tape. He put this in the box and
watched as the guard locked it away. The envelope
contained a stack of newspaper cuttings.

He left the bank and drove to the motel where he
had registered earlier as Moorehead. On a sheet of
motel stationery he began sketching the bank's floor
plan. A rough sketch was all he wanted now. When he
saw Giordano's photos, the two of them could work
together on it and produce something more detailed.

He left the motel room. A beautiful day, he thought.
Perfect for golf. He got into his car and headed north
out of town, then cut west on Route 4. When he saw
the driving range, he pulled off the road. He took his
driver and his spoon from the trunk and bought a
bucket of balls.

He hit eight balls before he lost interest entirely. He
topped the first one, caught the next two nicely, then
sliced the rest. He left the remaining forty-two balls in
the bucket on the rubber mat and put his clubs back in
the bag and locked the trunk.

He drove another half mile down the road to a gas
station. The pay phone was set up for direct-dialing.
He dropped a dime in the slot and called Tarrytown.

Giordano hung the last of the prints up to dry.
There were sixteen of them and almost all of them had
come out sharp and clear. His camera was a Japanese
job about the size of a pack of cigarettes, and he had
loaded it with very fast film. He studied the pictures
now and was reasonably pleased with them. He had

enlarged the negatives to four-by-five, and could have made them still larger without too much loss of definition, but he felt they would do.

He poured his trays of chemicals down the sink and went upstairs. Helen Tremont was at the kitchen table reading a magazine. "Oh, Louis," she said. "I didn't hear you come up. You walk like a cat."

"I hope I didn't startle you——"

"Not at all." She smiled. "You're finished already? That was fast, wasn't it."

"The darkroom's a pleasure to work in."

"Yes, Walter spent hours on end down there. You've seen his nature photographs. He did some marvelous things. He always said it was the only hunting he cared for. Do you do very much photography yourself?"

"Not anymore. I did for a few months, but then I realized I had a cabinet full of prints that I never looked at once I'd developed and printed them, and I sort of lost interest."

"I suppose that can happen."

"And I wasn't an artist at it. I got to be competent, and then I never got to be anything better than competent, so from that point on it got dull for me. The only part I ever really enjoyed was the darkroom work. That's still a kick, you know, putting the film through the bath and seeing what you come up with. This batch turned out fine."

"Roger will be glad to hear that. He's upstairs, if you want to go up. Oh, what's wrong with me? You'll have a drink?"

"I'd like some coffee, if there's any made."

He stayed with her and drank the coffee in the kitchen. They talked about hobbies and travel, but Giordano had trouble keeping his mind on the conversation. When he was done with the coffee, he went up to the second floor and found the colonel in the library.

"The prints are drying," he said. "They came out fine."

"Good. I just spoke to Frank. He opened his account with no difficulty and managed to lease a safe deposit box. He had a look at the vault. No photographs, of course."

"His memory's almost as good as a camera."

"Yes. He'll be here sometime this evening to go over the photos with you. And Howard was on the phone earlier. They hope to get on the ground of the Platt estate tomorrow. They've laid the groundwork and should have something for us tomorrow night if all goes well."

"Yes, sir. Uh . . . as far as this evening is concerned——"

"Yes?"

Giordano hesitated. "Well, I did make a dinner date with one of the tellers. I don't have to show up if you think it's more important to meet with Frank tonight, but I thought it might be worthwhile to develop that contact. She's just a teller, of course, but she might know a lot about bank routine."

"Yes, of course." The colonel turned away for a moment, his brow furrowed in thought. "A dinner date," he said suddenly. "You only went there to change a bill, didn't you?"

"Yes, a twenty."

"And it was crowded, and of course the girl must have been rushed."

"Yes, sir, she was."

"And you still managed to date her?"

"Well . . ."

The colonel chuckled softly. "I see," he said. "I gather you'll be spending the night in New Jersey, then?"

Giordano fought against the rush of blood to his face. It was bad enough to be short and skinny and nearsighted. Why the hell did he have to blush? "She seems like a quiet sort of girl," he said. "I don't know, I mean, I——"

The colonel spun his chair back, wheeled himself over to his desk. "I think you're quite right, Louis. You should develop this relationship. A dinner date, you won't have very much time, will you? I could call Frank and suggest he make it tomorrow. No, that's not good. Will those prints be dry by the time you're ready to leave?"

"Easily."

"Good. Bring them up before you go, and I'll go over them with you so that I know what they are. Then Frank and I can work together on them. I think that should do well enough. You'll have a look at his scale drawing tomorrow. Just give me a call when you know where you'll be staying."

"The Cavalier Motel on U.S. One."

"Oh?" The colonel raised an eyebrow. "Did you take the room before you met the girl or after? You don't have to answer that, Louis."

Giordano blushed furiously. "I'll check those prints," he said, and fled from the room.

Ten

Manso started out at six thirty. He went to four restaurants on the list and had a drink at each of them. He drank Bloody Marys because he could drink them almost indefinitely without feeling the vodka they contained. He nursed each drink for about fifteen minutes, then left and drove the rented Plymouth to the next place on the list.

After four restaurants and four drinks he was hungry. The fourth restaurant was a steakhouse in Clifton named for the ex-prizefighter who functioned as its maître d'hôtel. Photos of other fighters covered the wall behind the bar. There were elaborately framed oils of boxing matches in the dining room, and the menu featured such items as Jake LaMotta Open Tenderloin Sandwich and Fried Chicken à la Sugar Ray Robinson. There was also a Jersey Joe Walcott Special, which turned out to be a combination of lobster tail and sirloin.

The fighter didn't own the restaurant. Like the three others on Manso's list, it was one of Albert Platt's places. He didn't really expect Platt to show up, but it seemed worth a try. From what he had seen of Platt in Vegas, he had a taste for night life and enjoyed being seen. Most gangsters liked to show up at their own restaurants.

Manso knew a lot about gangsters. When they flew him back to the States, he had close to three grand in his pocket and he took the whole roll straight to Vegas. He won the first three nights straight and had the feeling that he had found the only sensible way in the world to make a living. The fourth night he stepped up to the crap table of the Sands with $8,500 on his hip. By midnight he had run it up to twenty thousand, and at a quarter to three in the morning he had a fifty-dollar bill in his shoe and no chips at all in front of him.

An assistant manager bought him breakfast, told him to forget his hotel bill, and bought him a bus ticket to L. A. Manso cashed the ticket at the bus station. He took a five-a-week room in downtown Vegas and got a job in an automatic car wash. He spent every night at the downtown casinos. He played as small as he could and never lost more than five dollars in a night. Most of the time he watched.

He ate out of cans and saved his money. He talked
to people, he read books. He thought things out very
carefully, and he finally concluded that you couldn't
beat the tables, but he kept going to the casinos and
watching the play and betting nickels and dimes while
making larger bets in his mind. After a few more
months he changed his mind. You *could* beat the tables, but only if you had three things. You needed the
knowledge and the capital and, most important of all,
the attitude.

Even so, you weren't likely to beat the casinos'
brains out. But you could learn to tune yourself in,
could develop the knack of sensing when your luck
was coming so that you could ride the hot streaks and
go home the instant they cooled. You couldn't get rich
that way, but if you had a thick enough bankroll, you
could do about well enough to live fairly well without
working for a living.

It took Manso a long time to save a thousand dollars. When he hit that figure, he was ready. He went
back to the Sands. He was in the casino for eighteen
hours straight. He would make small bets at the crap
table, waiting for the feeling to come, and when it
didn't, he would kill time at a nickel slot machine waiting for the mood to shift. At three in the afternoon,
after sixteen hours, he was about three hundred dollars
ahead. He was also out of nickels, so he moved on
down the line to a quarter machine, dropped in his
only quarter, and caught the jackpot on the first shot.

He went straight to the crap table and pushed his
luck straight up to five thousand dollars. He couldn't
do a thing wrong. When his roll stood at five grand, he
had the dice rattling in his hand and a thousand of his
dollars on the table, a limit bet on the pass line and
another on the eight. He was set to roll when something happened inside his head, some message reached
him, and he held up in midroll and pulled both bets
back and dropped a five-dollar chip on the Don't
Come line.

"You're betting against yourself," the croupier said.

The dice came up ace-deuce craps. He cashed in five thousand and five dollars. He settled his bill from before and reimbursed the assistant manager for the bus ticket. He was on the next plane to Los Angeles. When the colonel called him, he was working on an assembly line at an aircraft factory and thinking about getting back in the service.

There was never any question in his mind about what to do with the proceeds from the first job they pulled. He had acquired two of the three necessities earlier, the knowledge and the attitude, and now he had the requisite capital. Now, with all of that cash in his kick, it didn't really matter whether he won or lost.

Since then he lived the ideal life. He drifted from Vegas to Puerto Rico to Nassau and back again. Sometimes he went to Europe, but the casinos there didn't have it for him. Everything was too formal, too stuffy. He liked the life in the American casinos. Plush, well-staffed hotels, the best night life in the world, beautiful and eager women, fine food, and action whenever he was in the mood. He won a little more than he lost, and when his luck went sour, he knew enough to stay away from the tables. He didn't need twenty-four hours a day of gambling. There were enough other things that he liked about the life.

The one thing he didn't like was the gangsters. You couldn't have gambling without them, it seemed. They were all over Vegas and the Caribbean. Manso knew some of them enough to nod to and others enough to drink with, and they knew him for a right bettor who didn't leave much on their tables but who rarely hurt them, either. They thought he was all right. He thought they were garbage, but he didn't let them know it.

Now, at Platt's restaurant, he carried the remains of his Bloody Mary to a table in the back. He ordered a rare sirloin and a salad and wondered if Platt would show up.

Manso was on his second cup of coffee when the gangster walked in. There were three others in his party. The other man with him was half a head taller than Platt and weighed fifty pounds less. His cheeks were hollow, his eyes deeply sunken, and he walked with his arms tight against his body and a look of incipient death in his eyes. The two girls were blondes in their late twenties, and Manso thought they looked hired. He watched Platt's girl and wondered if he had played the revolver trick on her.

He finished his coffee and signaled for the check. While he was waiting for his change he saw Buddy Rice at the door. At once he dropped his eyes, rested his forehead on one hand as if in thought. Platt had looked his way twice and had shown no recognition. Platt, though, would not be apt to recognize him; Rice, bodyguard and seeing-eye dog, was supposed to scan rooms his master entered and place the faces he found in them.

Manso raised his eyes again. Buddy was alone at a table on the far wall, positioned so that he could keep an eye on Platt's table. The waiter brought Manso's change. He left an unremarkable tip. When the welterweight-turned-headwaiter went over to talk to Buddy Rice, Manso got to his feet and left the restaurant.

On the pavement he lit a cigarette and walked off to the left. Rice had come into the restaurant almost five minutes after Platt. He had parked the car, obviously. Manso walked on past the restaurant's parking lot. There was an attendant on duty, a stringy kid in an ill-fitting uniform. But did he park the cars himself or just stand guard? Manso crossed the street at the corner, came back halfway on the other side, and waited. After a few minutes a car pulled in and the boy parked it.

So Rice had dropped them off. Then he must have gone on around the block to the lot entrance, where he turned the car over to the kid.

But when it was time to pick up the car, Rice

wouldn't have to drive around the block. For that matter, there was a fair possibility that Platt and his party would walk the few yards to the lot entrance with him. Whether they did or not, there was no room for Manso to make his play.

He stood in a doorway for a few moments, thinking it out. Then he walked to his own car, parked on the street around the corner. He drove halfway around the block and parked the Plymouth in front of an unlit house.

Another house two doors down was backed up against the restaurant's parking lot. Manso shucked his jacket and tie, left them in the car. He changed his black oxfords for tennis shoes and slipped noiselessly up the driveway and through the backyard. The lawn was soggy from a full afternoon of sprinkling. When a light went on in the rear of the house, he dropped flat on the wet grass, and for a thin moment he was back in Bolivia on an antiguerrilla patrol with high swamp grass bunched under him and the chatter of the guerrillas, a mongrel Indio-Spanish, rattling on either side of him. The light went out. He stayed where he was for another moment or two, then got to his feet and moved silently to the fence.

A bed of climber roses twining up a woven wire fence with the ends of the wire extending jagged above the top rail of the fence. The fence was chin-high, the mesh too dense for a foothold. He stripped to the waist, then put his shirt on again. His undershirt he rolled into a tight cylinder and placed on the top of the fence.

Then he got down on his haunches and waited.

Eleven

The sign above the door said LIGHT OF FREE-
DOM BOOKS. In the display window there was a vari-
ety of hand-lettered signs bearing quotations from the
Bible, the Declaration of Independence, the Constitution. Displayed along with a few dozen books were
photographs of George Washington, Adolf Hitler, and
a southern governor with presidential aspirations. A
bumper sticker exhorted the reader to support his local
police.

Murdock studied the display with interest, then
sauntered inside. A bell rang when he opened the
door. Seconds later the proprietor emerged from the
back. He wore a plaid cotton shirt open at the neck
with the sleeves rolled past his elbows. A tattoo on one
forearm read "My Mother & My Country." My Gawd,
Murdock thought.

He said, "How do. Just passing by and I saw your
window, reckoned I might stop in for a spell."

"Glad for the company," the man said.

Murdock sized him up. A tough old boy just a little
gone to fat, he decided, too much beer going down the
gullet and making the gut hang out, but a hard old boy
for all of that.

"Don't see many places like this up here," he said.
"All them so-called liberals, you walk a long ways to
see real folks."

The man smiled, but his eyes were wary. "Everybody thinks his own way," he said. "Free country and all."

Hills, Murdock thought. Probably a down-home boy, but then it was hard to pin a voice too closely nowadays. You'd hear them talk about the same in parts of Ohio, even Indiana.

"There's free and there's free," he said. "Down home they taught us between crime in the streets and thinking as you please."

"You sure do talk southrun," the man said.

"Tennessee. Hamblen County."

"Hell, I know where that's at." The hill accent was more pronounced now, the wariness gone from the eyes. "Rutledge? No, that's a county over, now. Morristown?"

"That's the county seat, all right. Now who'd ever figure someone this far north ever heard of Morristown, or Hamblen County either? Where I was, closest town was Russellville, and that was eight bad miles from us."

"Why, my folks aren't a hundred miles from there. Clay County? In Kentucky, just straight north and a piece west? Town of Gooserock, not that anybody ever heard of it that wasn't born in it."

"Don't know the town, but I sure know Clay County. Damn, I been *in* Clay County." He hesitated a polite moment, then extended his hand. "Hooker's my name. They call me Ben."

"John Ray Jenkins. Ben, you know Clay County, then you know what Clay County's rightly famous for. Now you hang on."

He went into the back room, came out again with a half-pint bottle about two-thirds full of white mule. They each had two drinks. Jenkins dropped the empty bottle into a trash basket.

"Some summer," Murdock said. "Hot already and hotter coming on, and you just know what's gone to happen when the heat of the sun gets to working on those nappy heads."

"Hell, you don't even want to talk that way in these parts," Jenkins said. He hawked, spat. "Okay for a nigger to break windows and shoot up the town and all, but a white man ain't supposed to take no notice of it or he's discriminating against his colored brethren."

"Hear you had a bad summer last year."

"Bad! Yeah, you just might call it that."

Murdock studied the floor. "Had us a bunch of good old boys down home knew how to stick together. It's a white man's country. What am I telling you, hell, Clay County and Hamblen County, you know what I mean."

"Hell, yes."

"Here, though. You don't even know who you can talk to, what with everybody who ain't a Nee-gro is some kind of Jew foreigner. Wouldn't of opened up to you without I sort of got the message from the window. You want to know something? Here I'm living not two blocks from them and never knowing when a riot's fit to bust out, and I can't go to a store and buy myself a gun. Call that a free country?"

"A free people has got a right to bear arms," Jenkins said. "You read the Constitution, that's right in there. Right to bear arms."

"Those do-gooders in Washington, what do they know about any Constitution?"

Jenkins extended his tongue, worried his upper lip. He said, "Say, do me a favor? Just turn the bolt on that door and tug the shade down. Won't be any business this hour anyhow. Thanks. You know, Ben, this ain't Clay County or Hamblen County neither, but there's still folks up here think this ought to be a free country. You come on back a minute."

The girl wore a loose-fitting African robe and a pair of leather sandals. Her hair was in a natural, a tight cap of black curls. She set three plates of food on the card table. The men did not speak to her or she to them. She left the room.

The smaller of the two men, whose name was Charles Mbora, forked okra into his mouth, chewed meticulously, swallowed. "Soul food," he announced. "Honkie got no soul. Honkie eats dead food, has dead white skin and a dead soul inside him. Dead heart and dead soul. You know how he stays on his feet?"

Howard Simmons nodded. "Steals our soul."

"Sucks it like a vampire. Our blood and our heart and our soul. They trying to kill us now, you believe it, brother, they got the gas ovens built and ready. What the honkie don't know is kill us and he dies. He lives on us, brother. We die and he starves. No blood left to suck, no heart to suck, no soul to suck, and the honkie, he plainly starves to death."

The third man, black as coal, fat as Buddha, said nothing. He had not said a word in Simmons' presence, and Simmons had been with him and Mbora for three hours, first in the coffee shop on Atlantic Boulevard and now on the fifth floor of a rat-infested tenement in the heart of the Newark ghetto. Soul food, he thought. The day they closed the deal on the house, he gave Esther an order: no black-eyed peas, no okra, no chitlings, no mountain oysters, and for the love of God no collard greens. *Colored* greens, that's what they ought to be called. "No nigger food," he told her, watching her wince at the word. "And I say that because that's what it is. Three hundred years our people ate that garbage because it was what was left. Everybody knew it was only fit for niggers. Mountain oysters —those are pig's testicles, and it says something about a man if he'll eat that kind of thing. Nigger food. You know what I want? I want my children to grow up not knowing what nigger food tastes like."

Now, he thought, it was soul food. It was black people's food and you were supposed to be proud you were black. He knew they needed it, needed this pride, and walking these murderous streets and seeing the homes and smelling the stench of the hallways—God, the stench of the hallways—well, they were welcome to whatever pride they could find.

Not for him. He had all the pride he needed in being Howard Simmons. He had such a soulful pride in his own self that he didn't need to be proud of being black or eating collard greens or listening to soul music. He listened to Ray Charles and Otis Redding because they were good, damn it, and he listened to Vladimir Horowitz and the Budapest String Quartet for the same reason, and he thought Mahalia Jackson was talented but boring and that Moms Mabley was a dirty old lady, which perhaps made him a prude and a square, but that was the way he was. He had his pride in his home and his yard and his wife and his children and himself and the money he made with his hands and his brains. That was pride enough for him.

He finished the food on his plate, though. He didn't like it and never would, but now he ate it and pretended to like it.

Mbora was saying, "And something else. Two men, and one is sucking the other's blood, and what has you got? The one is evil and the other is a fool, and the fool deserves the evil that is visited down upon him. The willing victim is as bad as the villain. Those Jews marching off to the gas chamber like sheep to slaughter, and there is niggers who will do the same. They do it now and they'll do it when it's not just the sucking of soul and blood but when it's death. Sheep to slaughter."

"Not this sheep," Simmons said.

"Everybody says. Everybody." Mbora stood up, clasped his hands together behind his back, lowered his head, paced like a caged jungle cat. He had protruding eyes that were even more prominent behind thick horn-rimmed glasses. Unlike the girl and the silent man, he wore western clothes—a three-button black worsted suit, a button-down shirt, a black knit tie. He was thin and knobby, and he reminded Simmons of someone, but he couldn't think who.

"You want to know something? You wonder why I waste my time on you?" A finger quivered under Simmons' nose. "Because two minutes of talking to you and I know you got a head on you. You got a brain in that head. You walk these streets and so many is so ignorant. From the day they're born they get told how niggers is dumb, and you tell a child this from the cradle on and they grow up dumb, they grow up with a head they don't know how to use. So when I meet a soul brother with a mind, I stay with him, I talk to him, I make my words drive that honkie poison out of his pure and beautiful black soul. You understand me, brother?"

"I understand you."

Mbora marched to the window, waved out at the street. "Down there they don't think. You start with men that think, that think right, that use their heads to think black, then you get them down there to follow. They'd follow like sheep to slaughter or they'd follow like an avenging wave, just so it's following with no thinking called for."

Who the hell was it he reminded Simmons of? He wished he could remember. It was hard to concentrate on the conversation without knowing.

"We shook this city up, brother. We'll shake this city up again. And other cities. This whole honkie state, and other states . . ."

The burnings made sense to Simmons. It was the same way in Detroit. There were buildings no one could save and no one would tear down, and the people who had to live in them were better off burning them, because empty lots were better than those rattraps.

But the killing and the looting—no. No, he couldn't buy it. All it did was leave black bodies bleeding on the ground. All it did was tell the bigots that they were right and black men were animals. Simmons knew what war was and how war worked, and he couldn't see the point in being in a war unless you stood a chance to win it. Vietnam or Newark, if you weren't going to win it, you ought to go home.

"You got a brain, brother." The finger in his face again. "But a brain by itself is not enough. You need something to go with that fine black brain. You know what you need? The man has said it. You need to go and get yourself some guns."

Simmons nodded enthusiastically. Son of a bitch, he thought, he didn't even have to drag the subject into the conversation. Mbora got there all by himself. And in the next instant he knew who it was that Mbora reminded him of. He was, yes, no question, he was a black Woody Allen.

Twelve

The girl's name was Patricia Novak. She was around twenty-eight, and Giordano gathered that she had been divorced for two or three years. She had two rather uninspiring kids whom Giordano had met when he picked her up at her house. Her parents' house. She was twenty-eight years old and divorced and she lived with her parents, and that just about said it.

There wasn't anything particularly wrong with her. She was just a little taller than Giordano, just a little too heavy in the waist and hips, just a little too broad in the face. A few months of substituting proteins for carbohydrates would cure that. What it wouldn't cure was the bovine cast to her face. Her features were all right, but Giordano knew that the features were the least important part of the face. They were like the jewels in a watch. What made a watch worth several hundred dollars was not the two or three dollars worth of industrial diamonds but the craftsmanship that went into it. In the same way, the beauty in a human face came not from its inborn features but from the personality that came through it. When a girl looked dull and stupid, it was generally because she was a dull and stupid girl.

"That was really one wonderful meal, Pat," he told her. "I never would have picked that good a restaurant myself."

"I didn't know if you'd like Italian food," she said.

"Oh, you can't beat it."

"That's about the best place around, everybody says."

Then everybody was crazy, Giordano thought. All pasta dishes should be *al dente,* not overcooked like a mouthful of mush. And the sauces—his mother would put a bottle of ketchup on the table before she trotted out a sauce like that. Well, everybody had always said Neapolitans couldn't boil water. The restaurant called itself the Breath of Naples, and that was accurate enough. The breath of Naples, he thought, was seventy percent garlic.

He opened the car door for her, helped her inside, then walked around and got behind the wheel. He wondered how many people held car doors for her. Stop it, he told himself. You don't just have to get through this evening. You have to string her for maybe a week, because she works in the place and knows the answers to questions you haven't even thought up yet. And if you're going to spend as much as a week fucking this side of beef, you have to sell yourself on her. Seducing her may not be a challenge, but you have to seduce yourself, and the first step is to stop taking mental potshots at the kid.

He started the engine but left the transmission in

Park. "I'll tell you, Pat. I was thinking about a movie."

"Oh, that's swell, Jordan."

Jordan Lewis, that was the name he'd given her. Very obvious and amateur, but he had one particular mental block—whenever he used aliases, he forgot them. Jordan Lewis he had used frequently in the past; he would at least be apt to remember it.

"I checked a paper, the movies. There wasn't too much of a selection."

"Every town in Jersey, they'll have three theaters, and all over the whole state they just have three different movies."

"They call it block-booking," he said. He decided it wasn't unreasonable for him to know this. He had told her he was an advertising salesman for a chain of country-and-western radio stations. "But the point is, Pat, none of the movies appealed very much. There was one at a drive-in, but I'll tell you the truth, I hate watching a movie at a drive-in."

"Oh, you don't have to tell me. I'm the same."

"You've got the screen way out in front of you and the sound booming next to your ear and it doesn't seem real. And then all the crazy kids you find at those places."

"You don't have to tell me."

He turned to her, a shy look on his face. "Any movie, though, I'll tell you, Pat, a movie isn't much of a treat for me. I must see three, four movies a week."

"You're kidding."

"What else do you do when you're in a strange town and you don't know anybody? To me a movie is part of being alone."

"I know what you mean. That television set, sometimes when I think of the time a person can sit in front of that box and just stare at it like a moron——"

"I know exactly what you mean," he said.

He pulled away from the curb, drove slowly with both hands on the wheel. "What I like, what I really like, is just to talk to somebody. And that's the rarest thing in the world."

"You must meet plenty of people, Jordan."

"But how many people do you meet that you can talk to? I mean really talk to. I mean relax and open up and talk."

"Look at all the people come into the bank. I know what you mean, it's the same."

She wasn't a bad kid, he told himself. Not a bad kid at all. The boxes people get into, the binds. She was okay.

At a traffic light he turned to her. He said, "What I'd like to do, well, I'm afraid to tell you."

"What?"

"Well . . ."

"You can say anything to me."

"I feel that," he said. "I feel that you would understand. But it sounds like—well, what I'd like to do is if we could just go back to where I'm staying and really relax and get to know each other. Jesus, the way that sounds!"

"But I understand."

"Do you?" The light turned. He pulled away, kept his eyes on the road but went on talking to her. "The loneliness, every day another city. I don't drink, but maybe we could get some wine. My father always said there's a difference between wine and real drinking."

"Oh, there's no question."

"What was that wine we had in the restaurant? I had it before, I can never remember the name."

"Chianti."

"That's it," he said. "We could get some and go back to my place. I know how that sounds but I'll tell you, I'm not much for parties and nightclubs, I don't get on that good with strangers. Listen, if this doesn't sound right to you, just say the word and I'll never mention it again. So help me."

He looked at her again, and suddenly the bovine look was gone, the stolid cast, all gone, and she had turned almost radiant. He wondered briefly if the change was in her face or in his eyes. It hardly mattered.

Then her hand touched his, a comforting pat, a squeeze. "Most fellows, if a girl agreed, they would take it the wrong way. No, you don't have to say, I know you're not like that. I think . . . yes. I don't care about movies either, Jordan. And I'm like you, and lonely, you don't have to tell me about lonely. Yes, let's go to your place, yes, I'd like that."

When Murdock pulled into the motel lot, Simmons was waiting for him. He opened the door and got inside, and Murdock spun the truck in a neat circle and drove back onto the highway.

"How'd you do?"

"Two pieces. Fifty dollars for the two, if you can believe that. Soul brothers stick together. He didn't make a dime on me."

"I got two and paid three times that. More. Ninety for the Ruger and seventy-five for the Smith and Wesson."

"Caliber?"

"The Ruger's a forty-five. Mean old thing. The S and W's a thirty-eight, takes the same load as killed that guard."

"I got both thirty-eights, but one is chambered for magnum loads, which I believe is what they took out of the teller that was shot."

"Lucky it didn't take her arm off, a magnum shell coming off a thirty-eight frame."

"Or take the arm off whoever fired it."

"You know it." They lit cigarettes, and Murdock inhaled deeply and blew out a cloud of smoke. "They'll know it wasn't the same guns, won't they?"

"Uh-huh. Ballistics. They can tell. But they'll also figure that a pro always gets rid of a gun if he uses it but that he sticks to the same general type of gun. What the colonel calls verisimilitude."

"Now what the fuck does that mean, boy?"

"Means you should wear falsies if you want people to think you're a girl."

"I'll just bet it says that in the dictionary. Right like that."

"Just in the unabridged dictionary."

"What I say, you teach a nigger to read and he just don't know when to quit."

"That's the truth. Rednecks, now, you don't have that trouble. Never yet heard of one they could teach to read."

"Well, now, you just know it's tough enough getting used to wearing shoes. You should have heard some of the things I said about niggers. And I got three, no, four new jokes I'll have to tell you."

"We're even. I spent a couple hours agreeing that honkies are the worst thing in the universe."

"What the hell's a honkie?"

"A redneck."

"I'll be damned, I'm a word I never heard of. What's it come from?"

"I don't know."

"Don't know where *redneck* comes from, for that matter. My neck ain't red unless I stand in the sun, which I don't."

"As far as that goes, I haven't nigged in years."

"Huh?"

"I say I haven't nigged in years, so why do they call me a nigger?"

"If that don't beat all." Murdock laughed, slapped the steering wheel. "Now, that's funny."

"Old joke."

"Never heard it. 'I haven't nigged in years.' There's a drugstore. You want to call Old Rugged or should I?"

"I might as well. I have to call my wife, anyway."

"What for?"

"I call her every night. You know, just to see how she is and let her know I'm all right."

"Yeah," Murdock said.

He parked the truck and waited while Simmons went inside. He looked at his cigarette for a moment, then pitched it out the window. Aloud he said, "Ain't nobody in this world I'd call."

Nobody at all, he thought. Just to call up and talk to, well, there wasn't anybody. Not that he felt the lack. But still.

But, he wondered, why did Simmons make a point of saying it? If he was going to call, well, fine, and go ahead and do it, but why say? Or was he just trying to make me feel bad?

Oh shit, he thought. Think on things too hard and you just went and made yourself crazy. And he looked down on the floor at the two paper bags, each with two guns in it, and thought where they all came from, and the too-hard thoughts went away and he just put his head back and started laughing.

It was like gambling in one respect. The important quality, the absolute essential, was patience. Hurry up and wait—that was how the Army put it. You had to be able to move fast. You also had to be able to go without moving at all.

Manso was stretched flat on his back underneath Albert Platt's black Lincoln. He had remained in that position for well over an hour. First he had crouched beside the fence until the lot attendant delivered the car. Then, with the kid in the car and the engine going and the kid down at the far end of the lot and facing out toward the street, Manso took three running steps and slapped his hands onto the bunched-up tee shirt and vaulted the fence. He landed soft, landed on the balls of his feet, and in seconds he was out of sight behind a car, the tee shirt tucked under his belt.

Another few minutes and he had found Platt's car. He knew the model and license number—the colonel's sister was aces in the research department. The doors were unlocked, the key in the ignition. He considered and quickly rejected the idea of hiding in the back seat. Instead he picked another good moment and let himself into the car long enough to pop the hood latch. He slipped out of sight then, waiting, and when the kid took a moment to duck out of sight around the front of the restaurant, Manso raised the hood and loosened a wire coming out of the distributor.

Then he crawled under the car.

He was still there now, forcing himself to remain alert and prepared without getting jumpy in the process. He played the exercise through his mind and couldn't find anything wildly wrong with the plan. The only drawback was his relative immobility. It was not particularly easy to get out from under a car in a hurry. Still, he didn't think that would matter too much.

He tensed himself at the sound of approaching footsteps. It was the attendant, he knew the kid's walk by now. And this time the footsteps did not turn away. The kid opened the door on the driver's side of the big Lincoln, and Manso watched the frame of the car settle as the kid got behind the wheel. The kid turned the key and the starter ground. Where Manso lay, the noise of the starter was particularly loud. He thought, for the first time, what an utter snafu it would be if he'd yanked an unimportant wire and the fucking car started after all. The car would probably run right over him, and he would damn well deserve it.

But the engine did not catch. The starter motor whirred and whirred and the car shook with the repeated vibration, but there was no spark, no ignition. Give up, Manso thought. Get out of the car before you kill the battery. Go on, you schmuck.

The door opened, the kid got out and trotted off. Manso gave him a few seconds lead time, then began inching his way out from under the car on the passenger side. He crouched at the side of the car, his feet hidden behind a tire. He saw the kid returning with Buddy Rice walking impatiently on ahead of him. The kid was trying to explain and Rice was saying that he was a stupid little prick and he must have flooded it and why the hell couldn't he learn how to start a car without flooding the goddamned carburetor, and it better start now or he'll just be wishing that all Mr. Platt does is get him fired, for Christ's sake.

Rice dropped behind the wheel and ground the starter.

"See, Mr. Rice? It just goes like that, pocketa-pocketa, but it don't catch. I thought——"

"Not flooded," Rice said. He hit the hood latch and was around the front of the car almost at once. "Get your ass over here," he told the kid. "Did you have this hood up? Don't give me any shit, now, I'll find out if you did. It's a big car, a great car, kids like to fool around with cars. You have this hood up?"

"Mr. Rice, I swear by my mother——"

"You got a match? Here, I got one, take this. Light it and hold it steady, for Christ's sake. I said steady, I can't see a thing."

Manso had the knife in his left hand. It was a throwing knife, a hiltless wedge of fine German steel. Knives with hilts were supposed to be better for combat use, but Manso liked this one because it was so easy to conceal. You could tape it to your arm or put it in your shoe, anything, and there was no bulge and nobody knew it was there. He had the knife in his right hand and his left hand was up a few inches in front of his face, the elbow bent sharply in front of him. He moved quickly, silently, away from the car and around in an arc that took him behind the two of them.

"Why, you little shit, look at that! You see that wire? You were playing around and you knocked it loose."

"I swear, I swear by my mother——"

"Fuck your mother," Rice said.

That was all he said. Manso chopped once at the back of the kid's neck, pulling the blow back at the moment of impact and slapping the hand at once over

Rice's mouth. The other hand, the one with the knife, was already in motion. Manso remembered a sentry in Laos, remembered other men who had died noiselessly, and even as the memory flashed in his mind the little wedge of steel slipped neatly between Buddy Rice's neck and collarbone, slipped neatly in, through the artery, through nerve bundles, neat, easy, like dropping a penny in a slot.

In and out and then the blade wiped back and forth on Rice's jacket while he lowered Rice gently to the ground. No time wasted checking the kid. He knew he was alive, and he also knew he'd be out cold for ten minutes at the least. He spun, ran, the knife again taped to his arm, the undershirt bunched in his hands. In seconds he was over the fence and running through the yard and down the driveway. He trotted to the Plymouth, started it up, and drove off slowly, resisting the urge to put the gas pedal on the floor.

Buddy Rice had been dead for six minutes when Platt found him. By that time Manso was ten blocks away.

Thirteen

Dehn came back upstairs carrying a small wooden salad bowl. It contained two scoops of ice cream swimming in chocolate sauce and topped with gobs of marshmallow and chocolate mint sprinkles. The colonel looked at it and wrinkled his nose.

"Good heavens," he said. "I don't suppose you're actually going to eat that?"

"It's a chocolate sundae."

"Yes, I realize that. Is that whipped cream? I'm surprised Helen had the necessary ingredients on hand."

"It's marshmallow, sir. And I don't think she did. I stopped on the way and put the stuff in the fridge earlier." He took a spoonful and smiled apologetically. "A sweet tooth," he said.

"It's a wonder you don't put on weight."

"I don't eat that heavily, sir. And of course I stay active. But late at night I get a yen for something sweet, about the way most people want a nightcap."

The colonel shook his head slowly. "Now, I'm sure I haven't eaten anything like that in thirty years."

"Want one? I'll fix you one."

"Oh, I don't think so, Frank."

"I'm an expert, sir. It won't take me a minute, and you can go over the drawings some more while I'm downstairs."

"I couldn't eat that much. Maybe a fourth the size of yours——"

"A small one, then. Be right up."

The colonel shook his head again, slowly, then chuckled gently to himself. He was studying Dehn's drawings when the phone rang. Dehn had taken enough correspondence courses to function fairly well as an amateur draftsman, working smoothly with T-square and compass, and the sheet of graph paper tacked to the large oak board would probably be a satisfactory approximation of the architect's blueprints of the Commercial Bank of New Cornwall.

It was Manso on the phone. The colonel listened for a few moments, replied in monosyllables, then put the receiver on the hook. He looked again at the drawings but could not focus his mind on them. He thought instead of life and death, of crime and punishment, of the endless parade of eternal riddles.

His Bible was on his desk. It was a large leather-bound volume, the cover rubbed and water-spotted.

many of the pages stained. It had been in the Cross family for over a century. He held it in his hands now and remembered holding it as a boy and marveling at the date on the title page. BOSTON: MDCCCLVII. 1857. When he first looked at it, the book had seemed ancient. Now he himself was very nearly as old as it had been then.

Exodus, the twenty-first chapter. "He that smiteth a man, so that he die, shall be surely put to death. And if a man lie not in wait, but God deliver him into his hand; then I will appoint thee a place whither he shall flee. But if a man come presumptuously upon his neighbor, to slay him with guile; thou shalt take him from mine altar, that he may die. . . . And if any mischief follow, then thou shalt give life for life, eye for eye, tooth for tooth, hand for hand, foot for foot burning for burning, wound for wound, stripe for stripe."

He placed his hands palms-down on the desk and raised his eyes toward the ceiling. He heard Dehn on the stairs, heard him at the doorway, but he did not move, and after a moment's hesitation Dehn went back into the hallway.

Cross flipped from the Old Testament to the New, from the Father to the Son. Matthew, V, 38-9. "Ye have heard that it hath been said, An eye for an eye, and a tooth for a tooth; But I say unto you, That ye resist not evil: but whosoever shall smite thee on thy right cheek, turn to him the other also."

The Old and the New, the Father and the Son. Was it a paradox?

The Son died young, he thought. The young are different, they see with different eyes, they see what ought to be. And he thought, while wondering if the thought was blasphemous, that had the Son lived longer, His eyes and soul would have aged with Him, He would have grown more like His Father. He would have resisted evil, He would have returned eye for eye.

Cross pushed himself back from the desk, coughed a signal to Dehn. The ice cream, he discovered, was a treat. Not something he would care for once a day, certainly. In fact, an interval of thirty years between such dishes struck him as about right. But it was undeniably a treat.

"Manso called," he said. "The bodyguard is dead."

"Rice?"

"Burton Riess or Buddy Rice, as you prefer. Arsonist, murderer, bodyguard, and chauffeur. Edward said there were no complications."

"That's good news, sir."

"Yes," Cross said. "It is. Let's get back to your drawings now, Frank."

"Oh, Jesus," she said. "Oh, Jordie, oh, Jesus, I never thought——"

"Me, too, Pat. It happened."

"I'd hate for you to think——"

"Don't say it."

"Because you know, a divorcee, some people think——"

"Don't even say it."

"They figure just because a woman was married once——"

"Pat," he said. He put a hand on her shoulder, ran it slowly down the side of her body. She had too much flesh on her and Giordano didn't like that, but her skin was wonderful, soft and smooth and perfect in texture. "Pat, it happened. It was clean and natural and good and I'm glad it happened. We're a couple of lonely people, Pat. We needed each other and we found each other and it was good."

"Oh."

"It was good for you, wasn't it, baby?"

"It was so good I'm ashamed, that's how good it was."

"Don't be ashamed. You're a healthy woman, Pat. Patricia."

"I never liked that name."

"You mean Patricia?"

"I never cared for it. It sounded, you know, prissy."

"Listen, how'd you like to grow up with a handle like Jordan?"

"Oh, it's got character, it's very strong and dignified both at once. Jordan. It's a fine name."

"Character and dignified isn't such a bargain when you're a skinny kid."

"Don't say skinny." She touched him. "I wish I was built like you."

"That's a hell of a thought. You wouldn't have these."

"Oh, I didn't mean. Oh. Oh, Jesus, don't. Oh, I don't think——"

He kissed her, and she resisted for just an instant and then responded wildly, her arms tight around him, her tongue urgent in his mouth. He moved over her and her full thighs parted for him and he entered her at once, slipped softly home, and she lay back, eyes closed and teeth clenched, and moaned once and then sighed in the sweet luxury of orgasm.

He moved within her, slowly, stroking, stroking, and twice more he made her gasp and cry out until at last he felt that precious tickle in his loins. And then, as it came upon him, he was clinging to her breasts and hammering his loins into hers and crying out, shouting "Yes, yes, now, now, *yes!*"

As he drove her home she told him that he made her feel like a goddess. "Never like this, never before. Oh, Jordan."

She looked prettier now. Good medicine, he thought. Not so much the sex, that wasn't what did it, or else every jerkoff kid would be Mr. America. It was the romance that did it. Caring, feeling, relating, it all made her look more like a woman and less like Elsie Borden.

"You turn right at the next corner. I wish I didn't have to go home. That house. I wish we could have slept together all night long. Oh, listen to me, just listen, I sound like a whore."

"Not you. Not my Patricia."

"The way you say it I like my name. You make it sound like I'm a queen."

"Did I, uh, make you happy?"

"God, yes. I didn't, I haven't, I'm not, oh——"

"Don't talk."

"It's the next right and then a left."

"I know."

She settled her head on his shoulder and closed her eyes. This was the difficult part for him largely, because it was a departure from the normal course of events. Ordinarily now he would be trying to cool it with her, to set her up gently so that she would not be inordinately surprised when he didn't call her again. And, ordinarily, he certainly wouldn't call her again. She wasn't bad in bed but then she wasn't very good either, long on passion and short on technique. He knew, too, that she would improve even while he was losing interest. Her marriage had probably been less than spectacular in the hay—he would be hearing all about it before long, he supposed—and since then she had probably had a half dozen unsatisfying tumbles with no love lost on either side.

Men were stupid, he thought. They read books and learned tricks, they studied charts of erogenous zones like navigators plotting courses. They thought the whole point was to turn the girl on, to get her hot and then tuck her into the rack. That was the hard way and it didn't pay. The thing to do, the right thing, was to get the girl to fall in love with you. Not by kissing or petting or blowing in ears, but with words and tone of voice and facial expression.

Once they were in love, you were home. Once they were in love, they turned themselves on, they got themselves hot.

They neared her house. He slowed the car and she stirred and opened her eyes. He kissed her gently on her mouth.

He said, "Tomorrow . . ."

During

Platt was wearing a maroon silk dressing gown imported from Italy. It was monogrammed over the heart—𝒜 J 𝒫. Platt had no middle name, but what kind of a monogram was A P? It looked like a newspaper wire service, a supermarket chain.

He tightened the belt of the dressing gown and slipped his small feet into soft deerskin slippers. He got up from the edge of the bed and turned to look down at Marlene. Her eyes were closed, her breathing regular as in sleep, but he knew damned well she wasn't asleep. She always pulled that after he screwed her. Before it didn't matter, she was his wife and when he wanted her he would slap her awake if he had to. But afterward, after she had gone to the bathroom to scrub his seed away, she seemed to slip into a coma on the way back to the bed. As if she would do anything to avoid being with him at such times.

Usually it didn't matter to him. Usually he was asleep himself before she returned to the bedroom. But now and then there were nights when he couldn't sleep, nights like this one, and at those times her feigned sleep infuriated him.

He looked at her. He pulled the sheet down, looked at the outlines of her back and buttocks under the nightgown. She still didn't move. He dropped the sheet in place.

Even in sleep, or what passed for sleep, the class showed. The rich dark hair, the white neck, the clean sharp features. It was the class that made him want to marry her right after the Lobster died, when he was sitting very pretty and in the mood for the class house and the class wife to go with it. It was the class that kept him from kicking her out on her little round ass, and, perversely, it was the class that made him hate her. She had no right to it, damn it. She was nobody, she was Marlene Pivnick from Ocean Parkway, and what the hell kind of class was Ocean Parkway?

He looked at her again. He said, "Sleep well, you cunt," and left the bedroom.

In robe and slippers he walked out of the house and around to the back. He hadn't taken twenty steps before a high-powered flashlight picked him up. "Take it easy," he said. "It's me."

"Sorry to bother you, Mr. Platt."

"No bother, kid. You're a good kid, you keep your eyes open."

He walked on, not even bothering to wonder which of the four nightshift guards it was. He liked that, guards on duty all the time. Longostini had the same setup and hated it, said it made him feel like he was living under a sword. Everybody lived under a sword, for Christ's sake. Everybody, bar none. And if you were somebody, if you had it made, you took precautions. It made him feel good, like he was the president, like he had his own little secret service.

He walked on to where a patch of sod had been cut and replaced just a few hours earlier. No headstone, no casket, nothing, just Buddy Rice in the ground with the lid shoveled on, Buddy Rice waiting for the worms to eat him. What did a dead man need with headstones and caskets?

When somebody got one of yours, you didn't call cops, you didn't phone the newspapers. You put him away privately before the body was cold.

He shook his head, remembering. The stupid kid couldn't have done it, there was no way. The punk swore Buddy knocked him out, which didn't make sense, but anyway there was no knife around and somebody sure as hell did it with a knife and knives don't walk away.

But what a goddamned mess. First putting the two broads in a car and sending them the hell home, which was why he had had to throw it to bitch Marlene when he'd been planning on taking those blondes both at once, since Kohler wasn't up to that scene anymore. Kohler was too busy dying to take an interest, he only wanted the tail around for decorative purposes. And Kohler almost died ahead of schedule, shaken by the sight of Buddy, and he had had to send Kohler home in another car and then call still another car with a couple of strong boys in it to get Buddy the hell home and under the ground before some idiot cop stuck his nose in.

He took a cigar from his pocket, unwrapped it, tucked the cellophane back in the pocket, flicked his lighter, and got the thing going. You could barely see the seams where they cut the sod. Once you were done, you were gone forever, gone all the way, and you couldn't ask to be remembered. Buddy was with him how long? Say ten years at the inside, and as soon as the last chunk of sod was stamped down, one of the boys was at Platt's side with hopes in his eyes.

Saying, "Mr. Platt, Buddy was a friend of mine, but you're gonna need somebody to do your driving and all, well, say the word."

"You a good driver?"

"And a mechanic, Mr. Platt. I fixed the Lincoln before we shot out here, it didn't take me three minutes."

"You're Gleason, aren't you?"

"Lester Gleason, Mr. Platt."

"You got anybody? Wife, kids, steady pussy?"

"No, sir."

"Mother, father, aunt you gotta see every third Wednesday?"

"Nobody."

"Buddy Gleason."

"Lester, Mr. Platt. Or Les, or——"

"Buddy Gleason. Right?"

"Yes, sir, Mr. Platt."

"Buddy."

"Yes, sir."

"A room on the first floor. Buddy's things, you keep what you want, the rest you get rid of. You sleep there tonight."

"Yes, sir, Mr. Platt."

Ten years minimum, and that was how long it took to replace Buddy Rice. This Gleason, this Buddy Gleason, he could be good or he could be not so good. He'd find out soon enough. He might drive too fast like so many of them did. They tried to show how good they were and they drove you faster than you wanted to go. Or he might not be good with a gun, or he might not know how to keep his mouth shut in front of broads or business people. That was one thing that was good about Buddy, the other Buddy. He knew when to shut up and he looked almost human in a suit. This new Buddy, well, he'd do until something better turned up.

But who killed him? Platt didn't know, didn't especially care. Gleason, maybe; he was horny enough for the job. If that was so, then he'd probably be good. Whoever did it, it was somebody in the organization, probably somebody in Platt's own part of the organization. It was very goddamned professional—gaffing the car to set Buddy up, then taking Buddy out with a knife. Buddy himself had been good with a knife and it would take somebody very good to do him that way.

Woman trouble, he guessed. Something like that. One way or another Buddy stepped on somebody's toes, and the somebody did the job himself or more likely hired it done, and the hit was carried out in such a way that there was no mess with cops. It was, all in all, a very clean kill to straighten up after. Platt decided he ought to be grateful.

The sky was light by the time he got back into the house. No sleep at all, and he wouldn't be able to sleep now, and Saturday night was always big. The things you went through.

He went to the downstairs lavatory, chased two Dexamils with a glass of water. Then he woke up the colored woman and told her to make him some eggs and a pot of coffee.

He was still reading the paper when one of the boys called from the front gate. Something about the tree surgeons, the same ones who had driven up yesterday.

All he needed. Rice dead, and the aggravation with Marlene, and not getting to those two quiffy blondes, and now his trees were dying. Five hundred a month for gardening and his trees were dying.

"Yeah," he said, "send 'em up to the house."

Fourteen

The house was a two-story semidetached on Curline Avenue in Passaic. Kenneth Hoskins lived on the second floor. Heavy Victorian furniture framed a contemporary Oriental rug. Every horizontal surface held things—china dogs, woodcarvings, souvenir ashtrays. Mrs. Hoskins, a plump, bright-eyed grandmother type, had obviously decided what would go where. Mr. Hoskins, a sixtyish Dagwood Bumstead, had obviously never objected to anything, and never would.

Now he said, "I've told this story so many times, you see. Over and over and over. Of course I felt terrible about Fred, that was Fred Youngwood, the guard that was shot? I felt just awful, we all did, and Alice, but at least they say she'll be all right, and there's the medical coverage, and I think other damages she's entitled to. I mean Alice Fullmer, the teller, she was shot also?"

Dehn wondered why some people turned statements into questions, and what they expected you to do about it. He nodded, which seemed to be what Hoskins wanted.

"I've been with the police, oh, I don't know how many times. The police here and also the state troopers, and there was the FBI."

"They came to the house," Mrs. Hoskins put in, "and several times Arnold had to go to them. That didn't seem right. Arnold works long hours."

"I had to look at pictures," Hoskins said. "So many pictures." He thought for a moment. "Books and books of them? Of criminals?"

Dehn nodded twice. "I certainly hate to take up your time," he said. "Especially on a beautiful day like today."

"It's their garden," Mrs. Hoskins said.

"Pardon?"

"Downstairs. They own it, it's their garden. Where we used to live we'd spend a day like today working in the yard, but it was too big a place with the children grown and moved away, and here we just rent and it's their garden."

Her husband said, "The people downstairs? The owners?"

"Yes." Dehn drew a breath. "But my editors like a fresh approach, you understand. Going straight to the actual eyewitnesses. This seems like an interesting case, no suspects identified to date——"

"You told me the magazine, but I forgot."

"*Factual Detective,*" Dehn said.

"I think I know that one."

"One of the leaders in the field. Now I have some sketches here, and——"

Mrs. Hoskins said, "You work for this magazine?"

"That's right."

"I mean you get so much a week or what?"

"Well, I'm a free-lance writer, actually." She was a peach, Dehn thought. If he'd hit her on his encyclopedia route, he wouldn't even have tried to make a sale. He'd have excused himself and gone away at once. "I write pieces for them on assignment," he went on.

"So you get paid for what you write." He nodded. "How much?"

An old schoolmate of Dehn's covered crime news for a paper in Kansas City and did occasional free-lance pieces for the fact crime magazines, so Dehn happened to know a little about his cover. The magazines paid around a hundred dollars for run-of-the-mill coverage, more if there were good photos. But if he told her that, she wouldn't believe it anyway.

So he said, "I get reimbursed for research expenses, Mrs. Hoskins. So I might be able to compensate your husband for his time."

Hoskins' time turned out to be worth twenty dollars an hour. It was money well spent, and Dehn made a mental note to throw a little cash at all of the witnesses. Because Hoskins was getting paid, he kept his mind on the conversation and dredged his memory for the odd bits of detail that Dehn was interested in. Because Hoskins was getting paid, Mrs. Hoskins kept her mouth shut, and that alone was worth twenty dollars anytime.

Last night Dehn and the colonel had gone over the floor plan of the New Cornwall Bank until either of them could have drawn it with both eyes closed. It wasn't at all hard to come up with a decent line of operations for knocking the place over. But it wasn't just a question of doing the job effectively. They had to leave fingerprints. They had to make the score duplicate the Passaic robbery in enough important respects so that the dumbest cop in New Jersey could get the message. The newspaper coverage was thorough, but the colonel had pointed out the importance of primary sources. The little details that would make for instant recognition, a gunman's phrasing, the positioning of the robbers, these were the sort of trivial points that no one would bother to include in a news story or police report.

Hoskins, for example, had mentioned as an afterthought that one of the gunmen had had a wart on the back of his hand. It would be easy enough to putty a wart onto the back of somebody's hand, and the fact that the original owner of the wart might have had nothing else in common with the new wart carrier meant nothing, since no one person would have been present at both robberies. Police reports of both cases would mention that wart, and that would be a tag.

None of the original criminals had had a mug shot on file, nor did any of Colonel Cross's crew. A wart was a wart.

"I think that's all I can remember," Hoskins said finally. "Of course there may have been other things I said to Lieutenant Frazier, but he could tell you that. Unless you've seen him already?"

On the sidewalk Dehn glanced at his watch, walked over to his car. It was parked so that the license plates could not be seen from the Hoskins house. Lieutenant Frazier, he thought. Well, why not? It might look fishy if a crime reporter interviewed the hell out of the eyewitnesses and never even visited the police station. And the colonel always said that the best defense was a good offense.

The fool things you went through, Murdock thought. All of that time and energy spent talking old Mrs. Tuthill into letting them saw an old limb off her tree, just to have a name to toss out at Platt, and here the old Jewboy could care less. Maybe that was one of the good things about being a gangster, maybe you just never had to worry about getting taken by some small-time con man. But Platt, he never even let them get a word in about Mrs. Tuthill.

"All I know about trees is the leaves fall off 'em," he had said. "And if they die, you can't replace 'em, you have to put in a little one and you're dead fifty years before it's big enough to sit under. I don't want trees dying, not with the kind of money I spend on this place. You see the garden? The lawn? I got the best. I pay for it and I get the best."

Murdock hugged the trunk of the tree, put his foot on a branch to test it. He was some thirty feet from the ground, and he turned to flash a grin at Simmons. Simmons could climb if he had to, but he wasn't exactly at home in a tree, and it stood to reason that a fool who climbed trees for a living would move around up there like a squirrel, and Murdock could do this. Heights didn't do a thing to him. The first ten times he jumped out of planes, he shat his pants, and the eleventh time he didn't, and once falling held no fear, heights became quite comfortable.

The branch was sound, so he stepped up onto it and worked up to the next one, testing first, then making the step. At least he didn't have to saw anything off this time. They had told Platt that they wanted to go over the entire property and survey the trees, and then the boss could send them an estimate on the entire job. That was the best line they could have pitched him. Platt wanted everything perfect, all at once. He didn't care what it cost, just so his trees and his lawn and his house and his garden were the best he could buy.

Murdock climbed a few feet higher, took a look around. The tree was probably good for another couple of yards but he didn't want to push it. He had enough height, there were good openings in the branches, and he was far enough up to be invisible from the ground.

He opened the clasp on the canvas sack slung over his neck and took out the little camera. Giordano had explained it to him, and he had gone over its use again with Simmons earlier that morning. It was about as simple as it could get. You just pointed it and clicked the clicker and after you'd done that a dozen times, you popped in a new cartridge and started over.

He shot the whole roll, spacing the twelve shots around what they had taught him to call a 360-degree perimeter, which was an Army way of saying you did what a dog did before lying down, you turned around in a circle.

He opened the back of the camera, dropped the cartridge into the sack, and inserted a fresh one. Then, whistling softly to himself, he started back down the tree again.

Manso said, "Eddie here, sir. I drove by the house at thirteen ten. Our tree surgeons are on the job."

"Good."

"I was wondering when I ought to go in."

"How do you feel?"

"Nervous, but then I'd figure to be nervous, wouldn't I? From his point of view, I mean."

"Yes. Did you sleep last night?"

"Some."

"Enough so that you're rested?"

"No problem. Sir? I think I'd like to go in soon."

"Of course you don't want to rush things."

"No, but he's home now, and it would be easier with him at home."

"Perhaps. You don't think the coincidence might strike him as extraordinary?"

"Sir, whatever we do, we're hung with the coincidence. Tell a lie, you might as well tell a big one. It's the same as being nervous, anyhow. Now's exactly the time I'd figure to make my play."

"Good point." The colonel paused, and Manso was about to say something when he spoke again. "I'd wait a few hours. Give our friends time to finish their survey."

"Check. Sir? Just how positive are we on the background?"

"Well, Helen did a very good job. The vital statistics are accurate. He was at the right place at the right time. It could have happened. It's not the sort of thing that can be easily disproved."

"I figured on playing it uncertain. Reluctant and uncertain."

"Yes. Edward, if you'd rather take your time on this, I wouldn't blame you in the least. I'd rather you held off until you felt sure of yourself. A day or two one way or the other——"

"Could make a lot of difference. No, it could. And the waiting is the hardest part. I don't know Howard's schedule, Howard and Ben. I think fifteen hundred hours would be good. And if we overlap by a few minutes, what's the difference?"

"Well, that's true enough."

"So I'll figure to go in about that time. I don't know when the hell I'll be able to get to a phone, but if Howard gaffs the car, I'll be able to signal. So if you don't hear from me in seven or eight hours———"

"Be careful, Edward."

"You spoiled my line. I was saying if you don't hear from me, just start digging around in Platt's backyard. It's not that good a line to begin with, is it? I'll be all right, sir. It's just butterflies. I'll be all right."

"I know you will, Edward."

When Simmons had seen as much of the grounds as he could stand, he made his way back to the truck. He tossed his clipboard into the front seat, then walked around to the back. Murdock was on his sixth tree and Simmons could only hope he was about ready to pack it in. He was impatient to get going.

Something about the place gave him the jitters. At first the lawn and gardens had overwhelmed him. The plantings were what might be called semiformal, in perfect order and yet with a natural feel to them. As he walked through it all he had thought what a man could do with a place that size, the pleasure you could have.

Then another thought came along and soured it all. What was the thrill if somebody else did it for you? Platt, now, how could he take any pride in what he had? Somebody cut the grass and somebody else weeded the flower beds and somebody else trimmed the shrubbery, and Platt, all he did was write out a check.

Simmons had heard of stamp collectors like that. He was an unsuccessful bidder for one such lot, a prize-winning collection of German States issues that had taken honors at national and regional shows. The condition of the material was of an exceptionally high level, the mounting was magnificent, the degree of completeness most impressive. But the retired rancher who had owned those extraordinary stamps didn't know a watermark from a perforation. He had professional buyers purchasing stamps for him, and he had a commercial artist preparing his displays, and he kept the whole collection in a bank vault and never even looked at it. Finally he sold it because he got bored with it, but as far as Simmons could understand, he had never gotten interested in it to begin with. He was like Platt. He wanted the best, he could afford the best, but what he wound up with wasn't really his at all, because all he ever put into it was money.

Simmons opened the can of creosote. He dipped a hand into it, capped the can, headed over toward the garage. A short, stocky, well-muscled young man was polishing one of the cars, the Mercedes. He had already finished with the Lincoln, and it gleamed.

He said, "Yeah?"

Simmons held up a hand. "Wondered if I could have the use of a rag. Creosote, the can dripped."

The man waved a hand at a pile of rags. "Help yourself."

That wouldn't do; the rags were a long way from the Lincoln with the man in the middle. Simmons picked up a rag and walked along with it, rubbing ineffectually. He passed the man and approached the Lincoln. But out of the corner of his eye he saw that the clown was still watching him. "She don't come off," he said. "Y'all have some turpentine?"

"Beats me. I just started here."

Rice's replacement, Simmons guessed. From the looks of him, Manso would have his hands full.

"Ah'd look around," he said, putting the plantation accent on, "but Ah'd shore hate to mess up the boss man's things and all."

"Yeah," the bodyguard said. "Yeah, well. I suppose I could look. You said turpentine?"

When he turned, Simmons got the beeper from his pocket. It was two inches square and three-eighths of an inch thick, and it did something electronic that Simmons couldn't understand. He bent over and stuck it to the underside of the Lincoln's rear bumper. A magnet held it in place.

He was leaning against the garage door when Gleason turned to tell him there wasn't any turpentine. Simmons thanked him and left. There was turps in the back of the truck, and he used some to get the damned gunk off his hand. By the time it was all off, Murdock was climbing down from his last tree.

Fifteen

One of the guards said, "You got a package, hand it over."

"Has to be signed for."

"So I'll sign."

Manso shook his head. "Personal delivery," he said. "And it's not a package, it's a letter. It has to be signed for personal by Mr. Albert Platt."

"Listen, I sign for everything. He's a busy man, Mr. Platt. He don't have time to see delivery boys."

Manso straightened his cap. It was navy blue with a glossy plastic peak, and the badge on it said WELLS FARGO. Manso had bought the cap in a surplus store in Tenafly. He found the badge in the toy department at Kresge's. The cap cost $1.69. The badge was supposed to cost 29¢, but there was a line at the cash register, so he just put it in his pocket.

Now he said, "Look, it's only a job with me. I get my orders."

"So do I, fella."

"So I'll just go back and tell the boss I couldn't get through to Platt, and he'll get on the phone, and you can explain to him why you never even bothered to let him know I was here."

The other guard wagged the rifle at Manso. "You beat it," he said. "You just get the hell——"

"Hold it, Jack. I'll call, it can't hurt."

He picked up a phone. Manso didn't try to hear the conversation. The guard put a hand over the mouthpiece. "He says is it from Lucarelli or what?"

"Nobody told me a name."

The guard was on the phone for a few more seconds. Then he told Manso to get out of the car.

"I got to frisk you," he said. "Then we walk up to the house. The car stays here."

"Sure."

The frisk was cursory. The guard never even touched Manso's arms. It wouldn't have mattered if he did; the knife was now taped to the sole of his shoe. They walked together up the curving driveway to the house. The guard didn't say anything and neither did Manso. He had a manila envelope in one hand, a receipt book in the other.

Platt was waiting in the entrance hall. The man at his side was built like a fireplug. Platt said, "Okay, kid, go ahead," and the guard left the house. To Manso, Platt said, "What is this crap that I gotta sign for some letter?"

"Just doing my job, Mr. Platt."

"Yeah. Well, hand it over." Manso gave him the envelope and Platt looked at it without opening it, then thrust it into a pocket. "Now gimme your pad."

"You have to read it first, Mr. Platt."

"I have to what?"

Manso nodded. "What I was told. You have to sign that you received the letter and read it."

"Who the hell sent this?"

"They didn't tell me."

He held his breath while Platt tore the end off the envelope, drew out the single sheet of paper. He looked at Platt, then at the man next to him, watching one for his reaction while estimating the force and speed of the other. The heavy didn't look too bad, but Platt was a study. His face ran through a full range of emotions, registering surprise and shock and irritation and anger.

He said, "Okay, kid. Who's this from?"

"Me."

"You sent it yourself?"

"That's right."

"And the crap with the messenger outfit?"

"Just to get past the gate."

"What the hell do you know about Buddy?"

"I listen close, I hear things."

Platt turned to the fireplug. "Get this. 'Mr. Platt: I am your new bodyguard and chauffeur. I can do anything Buddy Rice could do. Also I'm alive and he isn't.' I'll be a son of a bitch." To Manso he said, "Just who the hell do you think you are?"

"It says in the letter. Your new bodyguard."

"Somebody put you up to this?"

"No. My own idea."

"Yeah, well, it's not the best one you ever had. The job's taken, punk. Now get your ass out of here."

Manso nodded at the bodyguard. "Who's he?"

"His name's Buddy. Scram, punk."

"Another Buddy?" He straightened, rested his weight on the balls of his feet. "I'll tell you, Mr. Platt. You want me to go, tell Buddy here to throw me out."

"Why?"

"Maybe he can't."

Platt stared at him, then suddenly grinned. "Yeah," he said. "Yeah, you do that thing, Buddy. Throw the punk out. You want to mess him up a little while you're at it, you go ahead."

Buddy hadn't shown any expression until then. Now

he came close to a smile. His hand dipped inside his jacket and came out with a gun in it.

"Out," he said. "Now."

"Jesus, take it easy! No problem!" Manso's eyes were wide with terror, and his hands went up in surrender, and as they did his right foot also went up in the air. Buddy was still looking at the hands and the eyes when Manso's foot caught his hand and sent the gun looping overhead.

Manso snatched the gun out of the air and pointed it at Platt.

And everybody froze.

"Bad," Manso said. "Very bad. I'll tell you, Mr. Platt, I heard good things about the other Buddy, but this one stinks on ice. Anybody who can't even hold onto a gun deserves what he gets. But the main thing is a bodyguard doesn't stand like a lump when somebody waves a gun at the body he's supposed to be guarding. Now what I would have done, Mr. Platt, is thrown myself between you and the gun."

Platt was nodding.

"And then, when I was in the way, I'd have rushed the gun. But standing like a lump, that's no good at all."

Gleason said, "Mr. Platt, all this prick is is tricky."

Manso ignored him. "And another thing," he said. "If my boss told me to throw somebody out, and the somebody was mouthing off that he could do my job better than I could, well, Mr. Platt, I wouldn't toss him out by waving a gun at him. I would want to make a good impression in front of my boss and show how good I could be without a gun." He turned the smile on Gleason. "You want another try, Buddy?" He turned and put the gun on a table behind him. "Ready when you are, tiger."

Buddy blew his cool. Manso had played him to do just that, and he was ready for it. Buddy came straight on with his arms out and his head down, and Manso leaned to the left and jabbed the bunched fingers of his right hand into Buddy's diaphragm.

Buddy doubled up and collapsed. He couldn't get his breath. Manso smiled at him.

"Now tell Mr. Platt you resign, Buddy."

Buddy caught his breath and got to his feet. His hand went inside his jacket again and Manso hoped it wasn't another gun and that he could be fast enough if it was. But it was a knife, a switchblade stiletto. Buddy held it low, blade up. He came on in a crouch, arms out in front, eyes wary.

"Now that's better," Manso said. "That gives me a chance to look good, Buddy. I appreciate it."

Buddy watched Manso's eyes. That's usually enough, but in this case it was a mistake and Buddy should have known better. He already knew Manso was good. With a good man, you forget the eyes and watch the feet. A good man feints with his eyes.

Manso glanced one way and moved another, and Buddy thrust with the knife and cut empty air. Manso had moved to his right, turning inward as he did so, and his right elbow dug into Buddy's solar plexus. Manso's left had fastened on Buddy's wrist while his right hand caught the man's arm just above the elbow.

Manso put his knee behind the elbow, applied pressure against the joint. The switchblade dropped to the floor.

He said, "He really stinks, Mr. Platt."

"Yeah. He does."

"Whether you hire me or not, Mr. Platt, you sure don't want him working for you. He's just no damned good."

"He's fired."

"Maybe he wants to resign. Buddy, tell Mr. Platt you quit."

Buddy didn't say anything. Manso increased the pressure and repeated the order. Buddy was shaking, and saliva dripped from a corner of his mouth.

"I quit!"

"Jesus," Platt said.

"You need him for anything at all, Mr. Platt? You got any further use for him?"

"I wouldn't let him take out the garbage."

"Well, then," Manso said, and broke Buddy's arm at the elbow.

He took Buddy outside, dropped him alongside the front entrance. He felt loose and cool. The conversational mannerisms he had adopted seemed to help; as long as he stayed in character it was easy to ride with the play. One thing was sure. He was absolute hell on Buddies.

When he got back in the entrance hall, Platt had the gun in his hand. It was pointed at Manso, and for an instant he thought he was going to be shot. He came perilously close to panic.

"I surrender," he said lightly.

"Who the hell are you?"

"My name's Edward. I suppose I'll have to change it to Buddy, but I'm not sure it's a good idea. I think it's a bad luck name."

Platt's mouth tightened. "You were very good there. You're as fast as I've seen."

"Thank you."

"Shut up when I'm talking. You're fast, and you played a long shot and you think it came in, and you're busy being cocky. You don't want to do that. I could shoot you right now and bury you in back. I could have you tied up and let half a dozen guys take turns with you until you told 'em things you didn't even know you knew. You get the picture?"

"Yes, Mr. Platt."

"I seen you somewheres. Where?"

"Vegas. The Desert Palms."

"You were out there? Why?"

"To have a look at you."

"For who?"

"For myself."

"Why?"

"I wanted Buddy's job."

"Oh, cut the shit."

"It's the truth."

"Did you kill Buddy?"

"Why would I do that?"

"I don't know, but for my money you just answered the question. You said yes to it. What's your angle?"

"I want Buddy's job."

"Why? God damn it, who *are* you?"

Manso hesitated.

"You said a name before."

"Edward."

"And a last name?"

Manso looked at the rug.

"You want Buddy's job but you won't even tell your name?"

"I didn't want it to go like this," Manso said quietly. "I thought I could start out working for you and then we could see where it went. I thought I could——"

"See where what went?"

Manso sighed, then raised his eyes to meet Platt's. "I thought my name was Edward Mann, Mr. Platt. For years I grew up thinking that was my name, that was me, Eddie Mann."

"So?"

"Well, now it looks as though my name isn't Mann after all. I've been trying to check on it, but I can't get anywhere one way or the other. See, the way it looks, my last name ought to be Platt."

He swallowed. "Don't expect me to prove it," he went on. "I can't even prove it to myself. But, well, you see, I think maybe I'm your son."

Sixteen

"Her name was Florence Mannheim, but she cut it to Mann when I was still in diapers. That was the same time that we moved out to Astoria."

"From where?"

"East New York. When she told me all this, when I started to check things out, I found out we lived on Pitkin Avenue. I went over and looked at the building. Nobody lives there now. All the windows broken, the door kicked in."

"Pitkin Avenue," Platt said.

"She always told me my father was dead. He died in the war, she said. Before I was born. She said his name was Edward like mine and he was in the Air Force and his plane was shot down over Germany. I checked that, too, and there was no record he ever existed. And Mannheim was her maiden name. She was never married, at least not in New York. There's no record of it anywhere. So I don't know if you're my father or not, but whoever it was, he wasn't married to my mother."

"Florence Mannheim," Platt said. He was no longer holding the gun. "This is crazy. I never had a son."

"She said she never told you about me."

"I never heard of a Florence Mannheim."

"She said you probably wouldn't even remember her. It was hard for me to follow her. She was dying. I was just back from the service and she was dying and she said she had to tell me something, and I said to just take it easy, just rest, and she sat up and started telling me that there was no Edward Mannheim and that my father was a man named Albert Platt. She said she went out on the Island and had me at a nursing home and the birth was never registered. I've never been able to get hold of my birth certificate. When I was sixteen, I had trouble getting a driver's license. I had to go to the school for proof of age."

Platt's eyes were half-lidded, his brow ridged. "You're how old?"

"Twenty-eight in February."

"So that's when? Forty-one?"

"Right. I would have been conceived in nineteen forty, say late May or early June."

"I'm trying to place this. A son. I never thought about kids, and then by the time I wanted one . . . I remember I picked up some kind of crazy dose. There was this Spanish kid infected half of Brooklyn. What we didn't do to her afterwards, Christ, you can bet she never clapped anybody else." Platt laughed, then was suddenly sober again. "Couple of years ago I went to a doctor. Specialist. He said that could have been what did it, that I can't have kids now. When the hell was that? I guess forty-two or three."

Thank God for that, Manso thought.

"May or June of nineteen forty. This is crazy, you're either a wise-ass punk or you're my kid, I don't know which. This is hard to get used to. Those years I was a nutty kid myself practically. Nineteen forty I was what? Jesus, I was nineteen."

"My mother was seventeen."

"Nineteen years old. Those days I would screw anything." Platt smiled at the memory. "We were wild kids. They used to say I would screw a snake if somebody would hold its head. What was it she told you? We had a thing going or what?"

"She said just once."

"One time?" Platt snorted. "How's she so sure I was the hero?"

"You were the only one. She said you forced her."

"You mean raped her?"

"She didn't exactly say."

"Yeah." Platt nodded slowly. "There were so many of them in those days. You'd pick up a girl and feed her a little booze and never see her again. Half the time you never knew their last names. Florence, there were lots of girls with that name where I lived. Only generally they were called Flo. Now it's not such a common name. What did she die of?"

"Cancer."

"That's a bitch, all right. Flo Mannheim? I can't make any connections. What did she look like? What color hair?"

"Sort of a light brown."

"And yours is dark. And the same as mine, isn't it? I'm a son of a bitch if this isn't the damnedest thing ever. I mean it's crazy."

Manso nodded. "It's been driving me crazy for months, ever since she told me. Either I have a father or I don't, and I can't prove it one way or the other. That's why I was sort of following you around."

"Checking on me?"

"Right. I nosed around here a little and then when I found out you were in Vegas, I flew out there and had a closer look. I stayed at the same place. I was right next to you at the crap table one night."

"You gamble much?"

"Some."

"How'd you do?"

"I won a little."

"Me, I took a bath. But what the hell, it's a vacation, you don't care. I got to sit down and think about this. You hungry? You want a cup of coffee?"

"Coffee would be fine."

"Come on. Eddie is what they call you, huh? Eddie

Platt. You know, you're a good-looking kid, and the way you handled that punk. Style. That's one thing I always had even as a kid, I had style. Who taught you to handle yourself like that? You learn it in the service?"

"That's right."

"Well, come on inside, we'll sit and have coffee."

Giordano sat in his car reading the resort and travel section of the Sunday *Times*. The newsstand got all the back sections a day early, and the newsie had told him he could stop in the following morning for the news sections. Giordano didn't think he would bother.

He was reading an article on new travel opportunities in Bulgaria. None of his customers had ever wanted to go to Bulgaria. It was not very likely, he thought, that any of them ever would. Giordano wanted to go there, though. Giordano wanted to go anyplace he'd never been.

He looked up, realizing he'd read the same paragraph three times over and had retained none of it. He propped the paper against the steering wheel and leaned back. His car was parked at a shopping plaza a mile and three-quarters from the Platt estate. The homing device that Simmons had attached to Platt's Lincoln had an effective range of five miles, and the receiver on the seat next to Giordano was turned all the way up. But there was no sound coming out of it.

The beeper was the type used by police to pinpoint the location of a moving car. In order to do that effectively, you had to have three receiving units in operation, using three cars in radio contact to triangulate on the car under surveillance. They only had one receiver, but it was really all they needed. Simmons had planted the homing device with the switch turned off. When Manso turned it on, that meant he was planted and all systems were go.

If he didn't turn it on—

A muscle worked in Giordano's cheek. It was almost five now. Manso had gone inside at three. About that time Giordano took up his post at the shopping plaza, and a little later Simmons and Murdock had shown up to pass on the film cartridges and let him know the beeper was in place. All Giordano could do was wait.

He glared at the receiver. When it beeped, he had to scoot out to Tarrytown to develop Murdock's films and have a look at Dehn's sketches, and it would have to be a quick look at that because he had a date with Patricia at 8:30, and while he didn't expect to be on time, he didn't want to keep her waiting too long. The more time he spent at the shopping plaza, the closer he would have to cut things, which was aggravating. Worse, the more time passed without a signal from Manso, the more chance there was that there wouldn't ever be a signal from Manso.

Suppose, he thought, somebody took the car out. Five miles wasn't all that far. All Platt had to do was send somebody out for groceries and he'd be hung up waiting for a signal that couldn't come. Of course if the car was gone—that didn't necessarily mean anything one way or the other. It could mean, for example, that Eddie was doubled up in the trunk and they were taking him for a ride to the swamp.

But looking was better than sitting still. Giordano turned the key in the ignition and headed the car toward Platt's home. He had been past the estate several times already and had no trouble finding it. The entrance of the garage was dark and he had time for only a quick look, so he couldn't say that he actually saw a Lincoln there. But there were three cars in the garage and that was all the cars Platt had, so it figured that one of them was the Lincoln.

More important, Eddie's car was parked in the driveway.

He went back to the lot. The receiver remained silent. Giordano tried to decide whether Eddie's car was a good sign or a bad one. He thought it over and came to the conclusion that it was about as significant as the presence of the Lincoln in the garage. It didn't mean anything much one way or the other. The only question, the question that couldn't be answered except by the receiving unit, was whether or not Platt would buy Eddie's story. If he bought it, if he bought just a piece of it, they were still a long way from home. But if he turned it down, Eddie was behind enemy lines with no bullets in his gun and his ass in a sling.

Giordano didn't see how he could possibly buy it. Oh, the colonel's sister had done a good job, no question about it. While the five of them were still on their way to Tarrytown she was checking death records at the Bureau of Vital Statistics, looking for a woman who had died within the year, a woman born in Brooklyn somewhere between 1920 and 1925. A woman who'd moved out of Brooklyn just before the start of World War II. A woman who left no husband or children. A woman, in short, who had been in the right place at the right time and who had left that place at the right time and who had over the years left precious few traces of herself.

That was the background, and the colonel's sister had made a good piece of work of it, but it remained nothing more than background, a stage set for Eddie to play against. The long-lost bastard son routine—when the colonel had first outlined it, sitting up straight in that wheelchair and pointing things out on a blackboard like a brass hat in a map room, Giordano had been inches from laughter. But when Old Rugged Cross asked for comments, Giordano kept his mouth shut. There were, after all, two things you didn't do. You didn't tell a woman her breath stank and you didn't tell an officer he had rocks in his head.

Which was not to say that there was anything wrong with the colonel's head. And the more Giordano had thought about it, the more he saw the good aspects of the plan. If it worked, it gave them a tremendous edge. It not only put a man in the enemy camp. It did that, and it put stars on the man's shoulders. All in all, Giordano liked it enough to be disappointed when Manso was picked to play the bastard son. It was the proper choice. Manso was right in looks, he talked New York, he knew racket people. Giordano probably had an edge in hand-to-hand, but the bit called for someone who could look the part, and if Giordano went in applying for a job as bodyguard all he would provoke was laughter.

He wondered, suddenly, if he had ever fathered a child.

It was a crazy thought, he told himself. Platt, yeah, maybe he could believe something like that. That was a generation ago, when rubbers were unreliable and only married women had diaphragms and not even science fiction writers had discovered the Pill. For Giordano the whole situation was entirely different. The girls he knew swallowed the Swinger's Friend with their orange juice every morning. There was a drugstore on every corner and nobody had to have a baby.

Patricia Novak, he thought.

Divorced, lonely, living with her parents. Was she on the Pill? He had never even thought to wonder because he had for so long taken it for granted that every woman was on the Pill. Not her, though. He was instantly certain of it. Not her.

Jesus—

You fucking fool, he thought savagely, Eddie's up against the wall and you got nothing better to do than worry if some pig has a cake in her oven. If she does you'll never even know about it. You'll be gone in a week, and New Cornwall isn't the sort of place anyone ever visited without having to, and you'll never see her again, and it'll be two months before she even knows she's pregnant. And what you don't know about isn't really there, unless you're fool enough to imagine it, you idiot.

He looked at his watch. It was 5:27. He found himself wondering what he would do if some girl he barely remembered told him she was raising his child. He supposed he would send money—the hell, you never missed money, it was so easy to get more of it. But how would he feel about it? How would he feel about the kid? And it began to dawn on him that the colonel had nothing resembling rocks in that head of his. The legs might be gone, but there was nothing the matter with the head.

At 5:31 the receiver next to him began to beep.

Seventeen

Frank Dehn said, "They came into the bank at different times and moved into position. Wore ordinary business suits and had their guns under their jackets. Must have moved on a time signal, two men on the tellers, one at the door, another on the bank vice-president. They took him downstairs and made him open the vault. Couldn't have been much of a problem there. Platt would have seen to it that they picked a man who was clued in and knew to open up for them. They cleaned the tellers after they hit the vault. Left the silver, of course. The teller got hers because she tried to be a hero, went for the alarm. The guard may have been window dressing. Hard to say. The idea is he tried for his gun, but he died with the gun still in his holster and according to a couple of witnesses he never even moved for it, kept his hands in the air all

the time. So either one of the robbers panicked or else
they figured to make it more authentic by scratching a
guard. They play nasty."

"Appearance? Voice?"

"All white, so Howard can drive. They used a stolen
car, incidentally, left it seven blocks away. What else?
A wart on somebody's hand, and the majority opinion
was that the wart was on the left hand of a tall guy
with a crew cut. A dark guy with a thin moustache; a
couple of witnesses missed the moustache, but the rest
reported it. Not much on the voices except the usual
garbage—they were menacing, they were bitter, you
know the way witnesses project. What else? The moustache was the last one out the door, kept the crowd
covered while the rest piled into the car. Car was not
on the scene until they started out, then moved in on
cue to pick them up. . . ."

Louis Giordano said, "Her lunch hour's twelve
thirty to one thirty, so if we hit it then, she'll be out.
The tellers have each got an alarm button on the floor.
They hit it with their feet if they get a chance, but
they've all got instructions to stay cool if there's a
holdup. They aren't supposed to take chances. Where's
the drawings? The buttons are here and here and here,
and evidently there's a wire running across here that
they're all hooked to. Hit that wire and they're all dead.

"Cash on hand remains pretty constant, as far as
she knows. A Wells Fargo car comes by every
Wednesday at two to deliver change and small bills
and pick up old bills and silver coins for shipment to
the Federal Reserve. There's not that much cash involved, though, so you can discount that part.

"On the vault, she doesn't know too much about
that part of the operation. The president is somebody
named Caspers, but he's out most of the time. There's
a vice-president named Devlin. I get the impression
that he runs the show most of the time. He has the

vault combination; she knows that because he's the one who opens up for the armored car boys. . . ."

Edward Manso said, "The front gate is clean. The rest of the fence all the way around is electrified from ten at night until seven in the morning. During the day he has two men on the front gate and one roaming the grounds in back, but there will also be odd hoods that sort of wander around when they don't have anything better to do. At night, from ten to seven, the force is beefed up. Still two men on the front gate, but others here and here and here. A total of five at night. At night there are alarms on all the doors and windows. They're wired to the front gate. We went out for air last night and we didn't go five steps before a flashlight picked us up. The night men have walkie-talkies connecting to the front gate, so everybody's in close contact. Marlene says she feels like she's living in a prison. At first I thought she was just there for the soft life, but now I don't know. I think there's a pretty big love-hate thing there. He's got some kind of emotional hold on her. Maybe she responds to his strength, I don't know. She was bitching about things and I asked her why she stuck around. I got a funny look from her and then a lot of silence. I maybe shouldn't have asked."

"You want to come out?"

"No. He's got the vault combination somewhere. I lifted his wallet and couldn't find it there, but there's a safe in his bedroom and I ought to be able to get to it."

"We don't need it."

"Call it insurance. Anyway, I'm in like Flynn. He bought the whole story. He wanted to buy it, he's excited about having a son. But we play it very cool. In introductions I'm Eddie No Last Name. I'm inside, it's as easy to stay inside."

Howard Simmons said, "The traffic pattern is fairly

steady. No parking in front of the bank. I can pick them up in front and run two blocks without worrying about traffic lights. Then a right and a left. Say we stash the second car right about here. We'll be on the highway before there's any chance of a roadblock. We take Two-O-Two and cross the state line at Suffern, dropping some of the boys off on the way. We switch cars one more time right across the New York line, then take the Thruway north, cross the Hudson at Beacon, come back down on the Taconic."

Ben Murdock said, "I got that old truck painted brown again and the right plates on her. Only hard part is the waiting. I feel ready to bust out. The guns check out good enough. This here throws a little high and this one, hell, you won't hit anything with it unless it's big and you're close, but shouldn't be much shooting."

Colonel Roger Cross said, "Thursday. Thirteen hundred hours. You all have your assignments and battle stations. Now let us go over the entire operational plan one more time."

Frank Dehn said, "I don't like it and I'm damned if I know why. You know what it is? It's too damned slick. It's easy, and when it's this easy, I sweat. It doesn't make any sense and I know it doesn't make sense, but I don't like it."

Everybody told him he was crazy.

•

Eighteen

"You see, it's so dreadfully dull here," Marlene Platt said. "As cloistered as a convent, but no other nuns around for company. I hope you'll liven things up, Eddie."

"I don't even know how long I'll be here."

"Oh, bullshit," she said. She had a habit of peppering her cultured, slightly affected speech with vulgarisms. "The prodigal son has returned. He'll live out his days with his handsome father and his wicked stepmother——"

"His beautiful stepmother."

"Thank you."

"And I'm not even sure Albert Platt is my father, Marlene. If it turns out that he is, well, we seem to hit it off pretty well, and I suppose he'll be able to find some work I can do. And if it proves out the other way, I'll get on my horse and ride off into the sunset. I used to love westerns when I was a kid. There were a couple of years when I don't think I once missed a Saturday double feature. I must have seen, oh, I don't know how many movies."

"You wouldn't do it," she said.

"Do what? See a movie?"

She tilted her head back, lowered her eyes to look at him. Movies, he thought; God, the woman was a collection of learned lines and gestures, all of it wholly artificial and poorly integrated.

He was unable to figure her out. At first it had bothered him, but after a day or two he stopped caring and simply wanted her to leave him alone. He had toyed with the idea of throwing a pass her way. Not, certainly, because he wanted her to keep him company in the sack. She had the looks for it, but he had the feeling that underneath that fine skin she was all cotton candy and feathers. But it had seemed to him that a pass would win whether it won or lost. If she hopped into bed with him, then he had a friend in the enemy camp. If she reacted the other way entirely, at least she would avoid him, which would simplify his life considerably.

Somehow he had never quite brought himself to go through with it. There was just no margin for error; if she went screaming to Platt, it would tear everything to hell and gone. By now there was no longer any point to it. It was Tuesday evening. In the morning—

"Ride off into the sunset," she said slowly. "You wouldn't do it, not in a million years. Nobody does."

"Well, I——"

"Nobody leaves this house, Eddie."

The words were chilling. He remembered Platt showing him around the grounds. *You wouldn't want to know for instance what's under that bush or what's next to that tree, kid. Buddy is over there. Just a couple of days and already you can hardly make out the seams in the grass. Go ahead, take a close look.*

"Nobody ever leaves. The life's too good. It's very comfortable being Al Platt's wife. I'm sure it'll be just as comfortable being Al Platt's son."

"But if it turns out I'm not his son——"

"Don't be a schmuck. He's very excited about the whole thing, as though you just came on the scene as living testimony to his manhood." She put her hand to her forehead, rearranged a few strands of silky black hair. "Now, Eddie, you and I both know you're a sharp boy looking for a soft touch, and it was a good idea you came up with, posing as Al's son. He won't even try to prove otherwise. You're too good for his ego."

"Marlene, you make it sound as though——"

"As though your story is a lot of crap? Well, isn't it? You don't have to answer." She stubbed out a cigarette. "You think I care? He'll go through the motions of checking the story, then he'll say it won't prove one way or the other but what the hell, you're like a son to him, and you'll stay with the easy living, Eddie, and you'll be here a long time before you realize how much it's costing you. You're what? Twenty-eight?"

He nodded. He'd leave in the morning, he decided. Turn the car back to the rental agency, then up to Tarrytown and he'd be with the rest of them for twenty-four hours before they hit the bank. He'd tell Platt he had to go see a girl in Philly, something like that.

"I was twenty-seven when I married Al. Five years ago."

He didn't say anything.

"Wait until you see yourself five years from now, Eddie."

He grinned. "Yes, Mother."

"No jokes. It costs, all of this. Could you hear last night?"

"Hear?"

"He brought a girl home last night. One of his whores. He took us to bed. The three of us went to bed. A nice little family unit."

Manso knew this. He had seen Platt with the girl, had heard the three of them together. Now he avoided Marlene's eyes.

"Albert does like to prove his manhood. I'm surprised he didn't ask you to join us. His son and his wife and his whore all together, and it would have been perfect, wouldn't it? Because I'm not his wife, not in my heart at least, and you're not his son, and that blond slut, for all I know she's not his whore. You should have joined us, Eddie."

He said nothing.

"I think I'd have liked that," she said. Her eyes caught his. "I think I'd have liked it a lot. Myths are very compelling, aren't they? Oedipus and all that. Eddie——"

"I guess I'll go have a cup of coffee," he said.

"Why don't you," she said. "A nice cup of coffee. Why were you trying to open the safe, Eddie?"

"Huh?"

"Oh, cut the shit, as Albert would say. The wall safe. I saw you."

"Just testing my talents," he managed.

"Come again?"

"A fellow once taught me how to knock off a combination lock by listening to the way the tumblers fall into place. I saw the safe, I thought I'd see if I could still do it."

"You have interesting talents."

"Well, you pick things up. Like another guy, an Army buddy of mine, taught me how to hypnotize people. Ever been hypnotized, Marlene?"

"Constantly. Does Al know about your talents?"

"I don't really know."

"Does he know you pinched his wallet the other day? You wouldn't take money, you're not that stupid, but you must have been looking for something."

"His driver's license. I expected him to be older than he said he was, and I wanted to check without being obvious about it."

"You'd better go have that coffee now."

"Sure," he said.

When he was halfway to the door, she called his name and stopped him. He turned. She said, "He won't be back for a couple of hours. He went to see the Greeks in Trenton. He never gets back from there before midnight. Take your choice."

"My choice?"

"Choose coffee and I tell him. About the safe and the wallet. He might believe you."

"And the other choice?"

"Me."

He killed time lighting a cigarette. His mind flipped through alternatives. Easiest and safest was to knock her cold and just go out. Platt was away and he could come and go as he wished. Or did the guards have instructions to keep him on the premises? He didn't really know, and it could be bad to commit oneself in advance.

Coffee or Marlene? He was almost certain that it would be at least as dangerous to accept her offer as to reject it. He had the feeling he was damned if he did and damned if he didn't.

"You can always have the coffee afterward, Eddie. Don't take so long to make up your mind, dear. It's not very flattering."

Nineteen

"Hit him."

Manso tried to tense his stomach muscles, but he didn't have anything left. He let his gut stay slack. The fist hammered into his midsection and he felt his gorge rising, tasted bile in the back of his throat. He was almost sick, but he managed to hold onto it.

"You bastard. I take you in my house and you go with my wife. Hit him again."

The blow was the same as the last. All of them had been the same, delivered to Manso's gut with monotonous regularity by one of the nightshift guards. Platt and two of the guards had dragged him out of his bed and down the basement stairs, and now he was tied to a pillar in a small empty windowless room. The guard was giving him a beating and Manso was taking it.

"My son. If you ain't my son, you're dead. You hear?"

He heard. His stomach was on fire, his legs rubber, his head pounding. Damned if he did and damned if he didn't, which was what he had suspected all along, because she was a crazy bitch who didn't know what the hell she wanted, and there was just no right way to play it.

"And if you are my son, then what? The son comes and screws the father's wife. What kind of son is that?"

The hell of it was that he hadn't. He had passed her up and picked the coffee. *I couldn't do it, not my father's wife*—it had sounded phony even as he said it, but at the time it seemed safer than throwing it to her.

"Al, Mr. Platt, Dad——"

"Listen to him, he don't even know what to call me."

"It never happened. What she said, it never happened."

"So why does she lie? Why say she screwed you if she didn't?"

"Your money."

"I don't get you."

"Your will," he said, desperate. "She wants me dead, don't you see? She wants you to kill me. She's afraid otherwise you'll split up your estate instead of leaving it all to her."

The guard braced himself for another blow. Platt laid a hand on his arm. "Hold it," he said. "You go on back upstairs, kid. We don't want to take it too far too fast, you know?"

"Sure, Mr. Platt."

After the guard left, Platt went a long time without saying anything. Finally he said, "Both ways it's solid enough. She could be telling the truth, and then you're a wise ass working an angle who hustled her into the hay."

"Why would I take the chance?"

"Because men think with their cocks instead of their heads. Especially at your age. But don't interrupt. She could be telling it straight. Or she could be lying for the reason you said, the money, and then you're telling it straight." He paused. Then, "You know something? Only one thing matters."

Manso waited.

"And that's if you're my son or not. If you're my son, hell, blood's blood. If there was a misunderstanding, we just call it a misunderstanding and the hell with it. If you're not my son, if it's either a story of yours or else your mother was off her nut, then you get planted in the backyard next to Buddy. Because if you're not my kid, what the hell do I care who screwed who or who didn't screw who and who's lying and the rest of it. You follow me?"

"Yes."

"Tomorrow and the next day I'll talk to some people and see what I can find out. I'll tell them to fix it so you're more comfortable, but you better figure on making do with this room for a couple of days. It used to be the coal cellar. When I bought the place, I put in a gas furnace right away. There was a chute behind you where the coal came in, I had them brick that up. I figured it would be handy, a nice solid room with no windows." He laughed, then broke it off short. "Eddie?"

"Yeah?"

"A couple of days and we'll know, see? We can forget about all of this and the whole subject never comes up again. The hell, the door locks, you're not going any place. I'll cut you loose."

Manso steadied himself. Platt cut the ropes around his ankles and wrists. He was ready to spring at the man as soon as he was free, but he didn't even get to try. As soon as the bonds were loose, his feet went out from under him and he slid down the length of the pillar and sprawled on the floor. He couldn't move. He just didn't have it.

"Yeah. You rest and take it easy."

"I got a date."

"What's that?"

"A date," Manso said. "This girl I've been trying to get to. I got a date with her for tomorrow night."

"We won't have anything that quick."

"Call her for me? Just that Eddie can't make it, so she doesn't think I stood her up. Would you do that?"

"I guess."

"I'll give you the number," he said. "Her name's Helen Tremont."

Twenty

The colonel sat in his wheelchair and massaged the stumps of his legs. Both of them had ached ever since the phone call. It had come at eight o'clock. It was nine now, and they were all gathered in the library waiting for the colonel to speak, and all he could think was that his legs hurt. It was psychosomatic, and he knew it was psychosomatic, but somehow the knowledge did nothing whatsoever to alleviate the pain.

He said, "It's obvious that Eddie is in very serious trouble."

He circled the table with his eyes and studied the four faces. They gave back virtually nothing. He thought at first that they were impassive, stoic. Then he realized that it was something else. They were merely waiting for orders.

But he was not yet ready for orders. He said, "At the very least, we are forced to assume that Eddie has been exposed. The illegitimate son facade was never designed to withstand long scrutiny. Eddie insisted that it had been completely successful, however, and felt it might be worthwhile to remain behind enemy lines until the last possible moment. Evidently he's been found out."

"We have to get him out of there."

The colonel raised his eyes, sought out the speaker. "Howard?"

"Sir. If Eddie's in there with his cover blown, we have to get him out. And the sooner the better."

Dehn said, "This phone call. You said it was a man?"

"Yes."

"But definitely not Eddie?"

"Definitely not."

"Meaning he conned someone into making the tipoff call. He could be dead already, sir."

The colonel nodded. His legs twinged, and he massaged the stumps again with his hands. He closed his eyes for a moment, absorbed in the pain, and considered the possibility that Eddie Manso was dead.

If you couldn't send men to their death, you couldn't command troops. This was basic and everyone knew it. A low-rank combat officer had to be able to take it for granted that some of the men he led into any action would not come back. A strategic officer had it even worse; he would sacrifice patrols and platoons and companies, knowing in advance that he was sentencing men to death in wholesale lots. You had to be able to do this without getting sick about it, any more than a chess player let himself mourn for a sacrificed pawn. It was that intimately a part of the game.

And yet this private war was a very different matter, just as the Special Forces had differed greatly from conventional warfare. When you had only a handful of men, a small elite corps of skilled operatives, you could not squander them as if they were a swarm of foot-slogging infantry. Instead you had to aim for a minimum number of casualties.

Now, in their private war, they wanted no casualties. Neither the profit nor the pleasure of destroying Platt's operation was sufficient compensation for the loss of a single man. If Eddie Manso was dead, the entire operation was a failure, no matter how much cash the bank held or how neatly they took it off.

And Manso was very probably dead.

And Roger Cross's legs were killing him.

"We have to assume that Eddie is alive," he said at length. "I agree that this is very possibly not the case, but we must act upon the assumption. We will break into the Platt estate tonight. The cover of night is of sufficient value to cover the hours we lose by waiting."

"And the bank? We still follow through tomorrow on schedule?"

"No."

Simmons said, "Then we abort?"

"No."

"Then what, sir?"

Colonel Cross folded his hands on the table in front of him. He said, "It is probable that Eddie will undergo intensive interrogation. If that happens, he will talk. This is not criticism of Corporal Manso. Some of you may remember the way some of our Asian friends taught us to interrogate prisoners. I for one will never forget the Montagnard lad who worked with us up around Duc Din Hao. A very quiet, soft-spoken boy. Well.

"Assume Eddie has talked, or will talk. Assume the plan is dead. We cannot do anything for Eddie, if indeed anything can be done, before nightfall." Colonel

Cross drew a breath. "It is now nine twenty-three," he said. "Louis?"

"Sir?"

"Confirm my memory. The Wells Fargo pickup takes place Wednesdays at fourteen hundred hours."

"Correct, sir."

"There will be four of you instead of five. The old plan is entirely dead and we have only an hour or two to draft a new one. We will make use of the Wells Fargo pickup, and the four of you will hit the bank at fourteen hundred hours this afternoon." He closed his eyes, his mind already at work, picking at the bones of the Commercial Bank of New Cornwall, probing its defenses, searching for a new way to open it up.

Twenty-One

The truck left Tarrytown at 10:47. Simmons was driving. He wore the same overalls he had worn during his brief career as a tree surgeon. Under them he wore a dark gray three-button suit and a striped tie. Murdock and Giordano sat alongside him. Giordano wore a conservative suit, a striped shirt, a black knit tie. He had last seen Pat Novak on Monday and since then he had not shaved his moustache. The two days had not had particularly impressive results, but the colonel's sister had contributed an eyebrow pencil and Giordano's moustache looked passable.

Murdock had the other two tags—the crew cut, the

wart on the back of his left hand. The wart was putty and could be flicked off on the way out the door. The crew cut would not be so easily dispensed with. Murdock had always worn his hair long, with a sort of pompadour effect in the front, and now suddenly his hair was half an inch long all over his head. It would be a long time returning to normal. But he wasn't going to be returning to Minneapolis, wouldn't be dropping back into the slot he'd come out of, so it didn't much matter.

Simmons drove south into Manhattan on the Saw Mill River Parkway and the Henry Hudson. He crossed the George Washington Bridge into Jersey and headed directly into New Cornwall. He stayed just within the speed limit all the way.

The truck was the same truck he and Murdock had used to case Platt's estate, but Platt would never have recognized it now. They had sprayed it brown and had hung a pair of cast-off Pennsylvania plates on it. The plates had the same color combination as the current New York plates, which meant that no cop would spot them as phony unless he was standing on top of them. It also guaranteed that the license number would lead the police absolutely nowhere.

The colonel had obtained the truck for another operation. It was never used and had stayed in the Tarrytown garage ever since on the supposition that a thoroughly untraceable vehicle would come in handy sooner or later. Murdock, who had worked now and then in auto body paint shops, had supervised its most recent change of identity. He had also done the lettering on the doors, identifying the truck as the property of Hedrick's Appliance Service Corp. of Staten Island, New York.

Then, in a burst of inspiration, he had covered the white acrylic lettering with a coat of tempera-based watercolor the same shade of brown as the body of the truck. When it was dry, he used a white watercolor to claim the truck in the name of Moeloth &

Hofert/Plumbing Contractors/Bayonne, N. J. Two flicks with a damp rag and the truck changed ownership just like that.

In New Cornwall, Simmons drove straight to the bank, glanced at his watch as they passed it. He said, "Just over forty-five minutes door to door."

"About what we figured."

"Right."

Giordano said, "Plaza two blocks up and three to the left."

"Too close, Lou. Something further off?"

"Yeah. Keep going straight, I'll tell you when to turn."

Simmons drove to a large shopping plaza just across the town line on the north. There were two supermarkets, a chain discount house, a bowling alley, a short order restaurant, a batch of small retail shops.

"Beauty parlors are good, Howard. I don't see one."

Murdock said, "Bowling."

"Oh, right. A couple hours at the inside, and during the day they'll be women. By the time they come out they won't remember where they parked anyway, and they'll never figure out how to call the law."

Simmons didn't say anything. He drove slowly through the plaza, up one lane and down another. Within five minutes a Dodge wagon pulled into a space and four women got out of it carrying bowling bags.

Simmons said, "That's a Dodge, Ben. You want to take it?"

"Sure."

The truck slowed beside the station wagon. Murdock opened his door, swung to the ground. Simmons circled the bank of cars and stood with the motor idling. The four women had entered the bowling alley. The lot was generally clear.

"Don't know what he's waiting for," Giordano said.

"Taking his time. Ben likes to get loose first. Then when he does get in, it's just a matter of driving it away."

"Yeah. I always figure the only time you're really exposed is when you pick up the car. Once you're away, you're clean for four, five hours."

"Which is why we lay doggo here and screen him."

"Uh-huh." Giordano poked between his teeth with the flap of a matchbook. "Howard?"

"What?"

"I'd like it a damn sight better if I were driving."

"Soon as Ben gets his car——"

"Not what I mean. I don't want to go inside. Her lunch hour's over at one thirty, and we don't hit the goddamned bank until two. I don't see how she'll miss making me."

"You got the moustache, which we're supposed to show inside the bank. Also I'm the wrong color as far as the earlier job was concerned."

"That's minor compared to her spotting me."

"Why? She doesn't know your name, does she?"

"No."

"Well, then what's the problem? Ben's starting her up. Anything on the right? No, ma'am, nothing at all, and off he goes just like that. Very nice."

"There were some more bowlers two lanes to the right. Drove up while you were talking. Maroon Ford."

"I didn't even notice. Let's have a look."

Simmons drove around to the second lane on the right. He slowed down beside the car. Giordano had a hand on the door handle, then straightened up. "Keep going," he said. "The one just came out of the door. She forgot something."

Simmons moved on down the line, eased the brown truck into a parking space. A woman in a magenta blouse and a pleated black skirt returned to the Ford, picked up a black calf purse, and headed toward the alleys again.

"Son of a bitch," Giordano said. "And here we almost struck it rich. Bet there was eighteen, maybe as much as twenty dollars in that purse."

"And the car keys, man."

"That's a point. You get spoiled using car keys. And every once in a while a key'll break in the ignition, and then where are you? Whereas who in hell ever heard of a jumper wire breaking in the ignition?"

"Very true. Lou?"

"Yeah?"

"You bugged about the teller?"

"A little."

"You call at a quarter to two. Call the bank. You're a doctor at some hospital and her mother had a heart attack and she's dying, so your girl should get her ass over to the hospital."

"Howard, you're a beautiful man."

"Gets her out of the way. I do believe we can swing the dime for the call."

"I repeat, you're a beautiful man. Excuse me, I have to steal a car."

The Dodge station wagon wasn't precisely the sort of car Murdock would have picked for himself. The engine and transmission seemed sound enough and the car steered easily, but somehow the car felt like a toy. He decided it might be the color, a pale blue, or the dirty Kleenex and miscellaneous kids' crap that littered the rear deck.

Not that it too much mattered whether he liked it or not, he thought. The odds were that he'd never drive it. There was a good chance, as far as that went, that none of them would be driving the Dodge. It was a principle of the colonel's that you never went into a place before you set yourself up to get back out again. You gave yourself more room than you needed and as much as you possibly could. If you were going to have to switch cars—if there was even the slimmest damn possibility that you might want to switch cars, even— then you borrowed a couple of cars in advance and stashed them in likely places. If you needed them, they were there for you. If it turned out that you never needed them, then sooner or later the local police would turn them up and send them back to their owners. It might make pedestrians out of the owners for a couple of days, but that was just part of the game.

Murdock drove to the corner of Alder and Summerwood. It was in the middle of a tract of new houses about three miles east of the Commercial Bank of New Cornwall. He parked at the curb in front of a vacant house with a FOR SALE sign on the lawn. He left the jumper wire attached to one of the ignition terminals. He slipped on a pair of sheer canvas driving gloves and went over the surfaces of the car that he might have touched. Whether they used that car or not, there was no point in leaving his fingerprints around. The government had accumulated enough of Ben Murdock's fingerprints over the years. They surely didn't require any more of them.

He unzipped his windbreaker, reached inside the waistband of his slacks. The .38 fit snugly in his hand. He checked the load for the third time, put the gun back where it belonged, and, fingers nimble despite the gloves, zipped up the jacket again.

He walked a block from the car. He turned, and nobody had taken any interest in it, so he turned again and pointed himself toward the bank. He had close to two hours to walk three miles, and that was a pretty slow pace if you were climbing mountains. In the middle of a damn city it was the pace a kid might walk if he was worried he might be early for school. Sort of two steps forward and one step back.

Much as he wanted to, he couldn't hold his pace down that slow. When he reached the bank building, he looked at his watch and it read 1:37. "Thirteen hundred thirty-seven hours," he said aloud, pleased with the cadence of the phrase. But he wasn't pleased with the time. He could enter the bank and fool around with a deposit slip at 1352 hours and not before. Which gave him fifteen minutes to kill.

He walked along Broad Street, gazing thoughtfully into store windows.

At 1:48, Giordano dropped a dime in a drugstore telephone booth and dialed the bank. When a girl's voice answered, he said, "This is Dr. Perlin at Sisters of Mercy Hospital. You employ a Patricia Novak?"

"Yes, we do———"

"Have her come to the emergency ward immediately, please. That's Sisters of Mercy Hospital. Her father was injured in an auto accident and he's not expected to live."

"Oh, God."

"You'll see that's she's informed at once."

"Oh, God, yes. Sisters of Mercy. And you're Dr.———"

"Dr. Fellman."

"Dr. Feldon. Yes, I'll tell her immediately."

At 1:52 Murdock entered the bank via the Broad Street door. He almost collided with a frenetic, wide-eyed young woman who was struggling into her spring coat and rushing out the door at the same time. He clucked to himself and walked on through to the customers' desk, where he selected a deposit slip and a ballpoint pen. The pen was attached to the countertop by a length of chain. A hell of a thing, Murdock thought. All the money they had in a place like this and they like to worry over someone walking off with one of their ball pens.

He wanted very much to laugh. But he hunched over the deposit slip and penned meaningless figures into the little boxes.

At 1:53 Giordano entered the bank through the Revere Avenue door. He stood in line in front of the third teller's cage. There were four people ahead of him in line. If the line moved too quickly, he would

invent some business that would make him head back
to the stand-up desk—to endorse some nonexistent
check or other. But the line was going to be properly
slow. It would have been shorter if Pat was on duty,
but now two tellers had to do the work of three and
that slowed things down.

Also at 1:53 Simmons pulled the brown truck into
the bank's parking lot on Revere Avenue. Now he, like
Murdock, like Giordano, was wearing gloves. He took
out one of the guns he had purchased in Newark,
checked its load, and set it on the seat beside him.

He thought, *Esther*, and for a crazy instant she was
there with him so that he might have spoken to her.
Then she was gone. He had spoken to her the night
before. With luck he would speak to her again in a
couple of hours, and she wouldn't know that anything
had happened, but there would be something in his
voice that hadn't been there the night before.

Or would there? Because there was still Eddie
Manso in that big stone house.

He lit a cigarette and waited.

At 1:55 Dehn stepped through the electric eye
beam. The vault guard appeared instantaneously. "Ah,
Mr. Moorehead," he said. "Now you're a regular customer, aren't you, though?"

"I guess I am at that." Dehn was making his fourth
visit to the box today. He signed the signature card,
rubbing his sleeve against it to eliminate the possibility
of prints. Then he and the guard went through the little game with the keys, using first the guard's key and
then Dehn's key to liberate the safe deposit box.

"All filled up with hundred dollar bills, I'll bet."

"Oh, just some torn-up newspaper. I'm just putting
up a front."

The guard laughed cooperatively. Dehn took the
box to a booth, opened it, removed the manila envelope, returned it to his attaché case, and gave the metal

box a quick wipe to rid it of prints. From the attaché case he withdrew an eight-inch length of lead pipe that had been wrapped first with quarter-inch-thick foam rubber and then with several layers of Mystik tape. His gun was in a shoulder rig under his jacket, the .45-caliber Ruger automatic that Murdock had bought in Passaic.

He hoped he wouldn't have to shoot it.

He unlocked the door of the booth and eased it open an inch or so. The vault room was silent. He reached into the attaché case a final time and took out a pair of sheer rubber gloves. He put them on.

And looked at his watch.

It was 1:59.

Twenty-Two

The Wells Fargo truck pulled into the Revere Avenue lot at two minutes of two. The driver stayed behind the wheel. The two guards, dressed in gray uniforms with blue piping, went into the bank. One of them carried a pair of cloth sacks. The other was empty-handed. As they opened the side door of the bank Simmons ground the starter of the brown truck.

He did this a couple of times, staying clear of the gas pedal so that the engine couldn't catch. Then he swung down from the truck, scooped up the gun, and went over to the Wells Fargo driver.

"Can't help you, buddy," the driver said. "Not allowed to leave the truck. Now there's a gas station on Broad and Ivy, that's two blocks down and—oh, shit." He saw the gun. "All we got is nickels and dimes, is why I'm all alone here."

"Shut up and turn around."

"Listen, it's their money. Not mine. Right?"

"Right."

"So what do I care about it? Right? I got a wife, I got a kid——"

Simmons hefted the gun.

"Oh, shit," the driver said. "You could tie me up and gag me, but I suppose it'd take too much time, huh? Look, do me a favor, don't hit too hard. Believe me. I should care about their money. I could care less, right? One little tap and I'll guarantee I'm out cold for hours. And I got a lousy memory for faces, believe me. And——"

Simmons knocked him cold.

Dehn was waiting when they came downstairs. Two Wells Fargo men and Matthew Devlin, the bank's vice-president and, according to Manso, one of Platt's finest. Outside of Devlin and Caspers, the president, it was unlikely that any bank employees knew about the racket connection. But those two were in the know.

Dehn opened the door of his booth the rest of the way. He emerged carrying the empty safe deposit box under one arm. The hunk of taped pipe was held out of sight behind his back in his free hand. He ignored the three men clustered around the vault door and turned over the safe deposit box to the guard.

"Now, Mr. Moorehead," the guard said, grinning. "Feels lighter, doesn't it?"

"Sure does," Dehn said.

The guard took the box, turned, raised it up to return it to its slot. Out of the corner of his eye Dehn saw Matthew Devlin open the vault door. "I'll have your key now, Mr. Moorehead," the vault guard said, and Dehn hit him behind the right ear with the length of lead pipe.

The guard fell forward, against the wall, and slid gently down to the floor. Before he got there, Dehn had the pipe transferred to his left hand and the Ruger drawn in his right.

He said, "Freeze. Nobody move."

The guards were very good. They froze on command and held that way. But Devlin made a try for the vault. Dehn got to him, shouldered him out of the way.

"Just cool it, Matt. Don't screw it up now."

"Who the hell are you?"

"Stay loose, for Christ's sake. Didn't Platt tell you about it?"

Devlin stared.

"Yeah, the same drill as Passaic." He chuckled lightly, then turned to the two Wells Fargo men. "Sorry, fellows," he said, and put them both out with the pipe.

Devlin said, "Platt must be crazy."

"All I do is follow orders."

"And why did you call me Matt? And for the love of God, why talk like that in front of them?"

"In front of who?"

"Those two soldier boys. You'll have to kill them now."

"Oh?" Dehn's eyes flicked to his wristwatch, then back to Devlin. "Why's that, Matt?"

"They heard what you said. They could repeat it to the police, you idiot!"

"They could at that," Dehn said. He heard sounds from upstairs, the sounds he had been listening for. "They definitely could do that," he said, "and it might give the police ideas."

And he shot Matthew Devlin twice in the face.

When the two Wells Fargo men and the bank VP had been downstairs for three minutes, Murdock stuck his gun in a guard's back. Just about that time Giordano was leaning over the rail of the tellers' counter. He held a gun on the two girls while with his other hand he used a knife to cut through the alarm wire.

"Clean out the drawers," he said pleasantly. "Don't stall—use the cloth sacks behind you on your left. Good girl, good girl. Now fill them up with the fives, tens, twenties, fifties, and hundreds. Don't bother with anything smaller or larger. Very good, very good."

And behind him Murdock had the guards and customers and two bank officers all fanned out very nicely. When the tellers had their drawers clean, Giordano motioned them around to join the party. He kept the whole crowd in place while Murdock ran the two sacks of bills to the side door to hand them over to Simmons. Then Murdock went on downstairs to help Dehn clean out the vault, and Giordano stayed where he was, keeping everything and everybody cool.

"Now don't anybody be nervous and don't anybody be a hero," he said. He kept talking gently to them, telling them that nobody was going to be hurt, that they would all be on their way in two or three minutes. He called the bank executives and the tellers by name, almost as if he knew them.

Like silk, he thought. In and out and everything smooth and easy. He had one tense moment when two muffled reports reached the first floor, the sound of the two bullets that Dehn put in Matthew Devlin. He hadn't expected any shooting, and his first guess was that the Wells Fargo men had tried to be cute. When a few seconds crawled by without any uproar from the vault room, he decided that everything was still going the way it was supposed to. A customer asked about the shots and Giordano was so loose and cool he told her it was just the sound of the vault being blown open. The crowd seemed to believe it.

He held them all in place. In no time at all Dehn was coming up the stairs, heading out the side door. A few seconds later Murdock appeared, also carrying a large sack. He headed through the crowd and went out the front door. By then Simmons had the truck out of the lot and around the corner, and Murdock flipped the sack in back and leaped up after it, and Giordano, gun in hand, started backing toward the front door.

Smooth as pie and easy as silk, he thought, and all of this with them one man short and working on a short-notice improvised plan. The bank was a piece of cake and that was all there was to it. They could have knocked it over with two men and a four-year-old crippled girl, all armed with beanshooters and spitballs. Unloaded beanshooters. Dry spitballs.

He double-checked to make sure the phones were all dead. He told the customers and staff to stay inside the bank for twenty minutes or they would be shot. He didn't expect them to believe it, but the moustached man at the Passaic job had thrown it in for effect, and it was about time they did something that at least vaguely suggested the Passaic job. The colonel's substitute plan had left out some of the subtler touches of the original operations program, but you couldn't have everything. If they got the money and got away clean, that was enough. The police could figure the rest out on their own.

And if they didn't, and if the FDIC paid for the robbery loss and the government got a screwing, Giordano did not, in the final analysis, really care. The colonel cared. The colonel got all hung up on questions of right and wrong. Giordano cared a little about right and wrong but felt that the most important thing to do in any given set of circumstances was take the money and get the hell out.

So he worked his way to the door, kicked it open, spun, took three steps onto the sidewalk, and the shit hit the fan.

Twenty-Three

It had been a rotten day for Pat Novak from the beginning. A bad night's sleep for openers, with the little one up intermittently with nightmares. When the alarm went off at seven thirty, it dragged her unwillingly awake, shaky and headachy. She had coffee and put an English muffin in the toaster. When it popped, she took a long look at it, threw it in the garbage, and made herself a second cup of coffee.

And she just couldn't take the bank that morning. The usual people with their usual nothing conversation (*How do you want the hundred dollars, Mr. Frischauer? Oh, make it two thirties and a forty, Pat*). Irma, on her left, was busy indicting another in a long line of patent medicines that did nothing for her sinuses. (*Hodestly, they say id the commercial that id draids all eight sidus cavities. How do they get away, that is what I wadda dow. Hodestly!*) And the other girl, Sheila, was driving her batty with her latest kick. She had gotten all buggy about astrology a couple of weeks back and ever since then Pat heard more about the stars than she really cared to. (*You're Aquarius, right? Let me find it here. Yes, here. Listen to this, will you? "A day of great contrasts, sharps and flats with few grace notes. Before you answer the door, determine whether it's Opportunity or the Wolf." That's a wonderful one, Pat.*)

If it was a wonderful one, Pat couldn't figure out

why. As far as she could tell, the best thing about it was that it meant whatever you wanted it to mean. Not that she didn't sort of believe in it. With all the people who believed in it, and they included plenty of intelligent people as well as dummies like Sheila, well, you couldn't help feeling there had to be something to it. The only thing was, she decided, that she didn't really want to find out what the stars held in store for her. She knew that life was going to be increasingly rotten. If you knew that, you didn't tend to ask for details.

At ten thirty she went over to the Greek's for coffee. In the ladies' room she checked her lipstick and found herself staring vacantly into the mirror. She couldn't stand the way she looked, so washed out and stupid.

For a few days she had been quite beautiful. She stood looking at her reflection that morning and couldn't understand it. It was the same face, wasn't it? Why should a fellow make that much difference in a girl's face? Why should liking a fellow, or even loving a fellow (if she did really love Jordan, and she guessed she did) make such a vast difference? Just going to bed with somebody didn't do it. It might give you circles under your eyes and take the worry lines out of your forehead, but that was about all. It didn't make you beautiful.

Jordan had made her beautiful.

He was such a shy little guy, she thought. But when they were alone together, the shyness went away and he was almost unbelievably strong. In bed he was resourceful and inventive. He had taught her to do things she had always resisted, even during marriage, and she had found herself not only doing what he wanted but actively enjoying it. Somehow Jordan had a way of making things seem all right.

She wondered if she would ever see him again.

Probably not, she decided. She was reasonably certain that he wasn't married, but she was equally certain that he had not told her the whole story. There was nothing she could pin down, just a hunch, an impression that something was being kept from her. He didn't seem the type, but she guessed he was one of those who had a girl in every town he worked in. And why should he come back to her? She was nothing special. He had made her feel special, but now the glow was gone and she was alone again and not special at all.

So she looked in the mirror, and aloud she said, "You'll never look pretty again, you poor bitch." And wiped her eyes and went back to work.

The rest of the morning was more of the same, and by the time she had gone out for lunch, she was ready to disagree strongly with Sheila's astrology book. All sharps and flats? She couldn't remember a grayer, deader, duller day.

Then the phone call came.

Her first reaction was blind panic. An auto accident, her father in the hospital, condition very critical—she rushed out of the bank and started to hurry across town to the hospital. It was only a few blocks away, and it was easier to walk there than to wait for a bus.

Something stopped her halfway there. Something made her pause at an outdoor phone booth to call her house. She wanted to make sure the kids weren't home alone, wanted to know if her mother was all right. So she dialed her number, and it rang five maddening times, and just as she was about to hang up her father answered.

He was obviously not at the hospital. Nor, he informed her, was her mother or the children or, indeed, anybody else.

She couldn't understand it.

She started to go back to the bank, then considered. Perhaps the message was supposed to be for one of the other girls. She made another call, this one to the hospital. She asked for the emergency room. She talked to several nurses and left the booth with the certain knowledge that someone somewhere had played a pointless and rather horrid joke on her. A really rotten joke.

She walked back to the bank, her heels clicking furiously on the pavement, her mind spinning with combined rage and guilt. What have I done, she wondered, to be so bad that it would make someone hate me so much? She approached the bank, saw the brown truck race around the corner and pull to a stop, saw the door fly open, saw the guard, Nicholson, scamper around the corner from the Revere Avenue exit, and saw, suddenly in front of her, gun in hand, moustached and bright-eyed, the man she had never thought to see again, the man she needed, wanted, loved. Jordan Lewis.

He looked at her and froze. For a second or two they were figures in a painting, incapable of any movement, and then she saw Nicholson with his gun in his hand and she pointed at him and shouted, "Jordan, look out! Look out!"

Then the shots came.

Twenty-Four

Giordano was almost fast enough. He was squeezing the trigger as he turned, and he got off one wild shot before the guard's pistol snapped three times. One bullet scraped his side. Another buried itself in his thigh and hurled him harshly to the ground.

Then Murdock was leaping down from the back of the truck, emptying his big automatic into the guard. Giordano felt hands lifting him, carrying him to the truck. Blood welled from his thigh. He put the palm of his hand over the wound and pressed directly on it. His brain reeled, he couldn't concentrate.

"The girl," he managed. "Knows me."

Patricia was still standing stiffly in place. The braver ones were pushing their way out of the bank, staring at her, at the dead guard. Murdock raised his pistol.

"Don't shoot her. Knows me. Helped me. Bring her."

Murdock hesitated only for an instant. Then he darted across the sidewalk and grabbed the girl by the arm. If she had offered the slightest resistance, he would have killed her with a rabbit punch, but she let him haul her to the truck and help her in back with Giordano and the sacks of cash. Then Murdock, too, was up in the truck and they were pulling away from the curb, the tires squealing.

Giordano went blank, lost some of it.

Then he was conscious of her hand on his forehead, her voice in his ear. "You'll be all right, Jordan. You'll be all right."

Giordano opened his mouth, but nothing came out.

"Don't try to talk."

His eyes went blurry, then came into focus again. He looked at her, looked over her shoulder at Murdock, who seemed faintly amused. He opened his mouth again.

"Don't try to talk, Jordan, darling."

"We fucked it up," he said, and passed out.

Twenty-Five

Dehn's car was stashed on Front Street, and Simmons drove to it first. The hassle on the sidewalk had knocked everything slightly out of kilter. According to plan, Dehn and Giordano were to be dropped in the open after stripping themselves of guns and gloves. Then they would find their own way back to their stashed cars and take separate routes to Tarrytown. Now Giordano had a bullet in his leg and there was a girl along to complicate things, and the shooting made the brown truck hotter than a stove.

Simmons said, "We make it up as we go along. Frank, grab that rag, wipe the outside of the door. Take it right down to the underpaint."

He checked the rearview. There was nobody on them, and the only sirens he could hear were blocks away.

"We drop the bread in your trunk, Frank."

"Check."

"And Lou, I figure."

"And the girl?"

"No other way."

"Uh-huh."

"Makes your car hot as three stoves. That's your own car, isn't it?"

"Yeah, damn it."

"Your own plates on it?"

"The whole bit."

"I wouldn't use my own car on a job——"

"Well, I didn't figure to be driving money or tellers or people with bullets in them, Howard."

"True. You better not run any red lights."

"Very funny."

"And count on shooting any cop who stops you."

"That certainly is wonderful."

"Uh-huh."

"Howard? That girl is gonna be a problem. Who is she? The teller Lou was banging?"

"Right. I thought Ben would shoot her."

"Should of."

"Never should have started banging her in the first place. Same as Eddie never should have gone inside. You know what we did? We got too fucking cute with this one. A nice easy touch and we had to go and make it complicated."

"You said the other day you didn't like it."

"But I didn't know why. Now I know. It was too cute."

"Uh-huh. Say, you want to take Ben, too?"

"In the car?"

"Yeah. Want to?"

"The way we tore it all, I guess I might as well."

The transfer went smoothly. In a matter of seconds Dehn and Murdock transferred the money sacks to the trunk of Dehn's car. There was barely room beside the golf clubs. Murdock strapped the still unconscious Giordano in the front passenger seat, then got in back with the girl. Simmons hopped down and finished cleaning the tempera paints off both the doors. He was back behind the wheel by the time Dehn had the car in gear.

Simmons waited while the rest of them drove off. The roadblocks would be up by now, he knew, but they wouldn't make much difference. The area was just too dense a web of suburban sprawl, with overlapping jurisdictions, infinite roads, and alternate access routes, and it would take several hours to seal an area effectively. The colonel had mapped out the money route, a safe passage which would be followed by whoever wound up carrying the boodle. Simmons had planned to go back that way himself, but now he had to find another way.

Which meant getting another car.

Murdock's, he remembered, was in the Rolling Acres development at Alder and Summerwood. He drove there and saw the Dodge wagon in place at the curb. The house was vacant, the lot overgrown, and this inspired Simmons to park in the driveway. The garage door was unlocked. He opened it, parked the truck inside, and closed it. He quickly shucked off the overalls, balled them up, dropped them into an empty trash can, and emerged from the garage in suit and tie.

Across the street a woman stood in the doorway staring. Simmons looked at her for a moment in puzzlement before he got the message. He smothered a laugh, then walked quickly across the lawn. He had to give the FOR SALE sign a couple of kicks to loosen it. He pulled it from the ground, carried it around back, and left it with the trash.

When he came back, the woman was gone. On the phone already, he decided. But not to call the police. Right now she'd be calling her husband, and then the neighbors, and after that she'd be on the phone to her friendly neighborhood realtor. With any luck at all, half the houses on the block would be offered for sale within the next two days.

And of course the people in them would sell them to Negroes. They wouldn't think twice, since a Negro had already bought one of the houses.

Simmons got into the Dodge. He connected the jumper wire and the engine caught immediately.

He started to laugh.

All he had really wanted to do was get rid of a hot truck. And what he had done was integrate the goddamned neighborhood.

Patricia Novak huddled in the back seat. She hugged her arms against her chest and tried to keep from shivering. It was warm in the car, but she couldn't seem to stop shivering.

At first she had tried talking. She didn't remember what she had said, something about Jordan, but before she had her sentence half finished, the huge hillbilly beside her set his gun on his knee and smiled broadly, and told her that what she ought to do was sit very still and kindly keep her mouth shut tight or he would have no choice but to kill her deader than hell.

She had not said a word since then.

But she couldn't shut out the thinking. It seemed indisputable that Jordan Lewis, whom she had abruptly realized she was in love with, was not actually an advertising salesman for a chain of country-and-western radio stations after all.

He was, it seemed, a bank robber.

A knot formed in her throat. All those casual questions about her work—for the first time she realized why he had asked them. And then, on the heels of that realization, it came to her why he had gotten interested in her in the first place. It was not, she knew, a case of his getting interested in robbing the bank because he had met her. It worked the other way around.

He only asked her out because she worked at the bank.

He only slept with her to learn what she could tell him.

She felt her face reddening and lowered her eyes, staring dully at the floorboards. What a fool she was! Obviously his name wasn't even Jordan. And how he must have been laughing at her behind her back!

But.

But, she thought, he had kept the hillbilly from killing her. The hillbilly had pointed that huge pistol at her, and Jordan had said something that made him change his mind. And of course it would have been easier for Jordan to have let the man kill her. Alive, she was a problem to them, a loose end.

Did that mean Jordan cared for her?

He must, she thought. She remembered his touch, his manner. Of course it had to have been an act at first (and she blushed at the memory of the first night, the shyness, the meticulously planned accidental trail that led to his bed). But somewhere along the line it must have turned real, or at least partially real. Or else why would he have let her live?

Unless, of course, they had decided to kill her later.

She shuddered violently. Everything was happening too fast for her and she was unable to react to it. She thought briefly of her parents, her children. She couldn't focus on them. They now had no reality for her. All of her sense of reality was concentrated here, in this car, with these men.

These bank robbers.

Jordan, her Jordan, was a bank robber. (And to think that she had feared never to see him again. "You'll never look pretty again"—talking to mirrors like an idiot.) A bank robber, a bank robber.

And she held on to the thought and blushed furiously; between her legs she was suddenly marvelously wet.

Twenty-Six

Giordano came to in a bed. He sat up and looked around warily. His memory was spotty and he wasn't sure where he was. Then he recognized a picture on the opposite wall. He was in a bedroom at the Tarrytown house. He checked his thigh, which ached furiously. It was bandaged now and the bandage looked competent enough. There was more pain on the left side of his rib cage, and he discovered another bandage there where the first bullet had grazed him. Giordano didn't even remember that he'd been hit there.

He decided he was in a safe place and in reasonably good condition. He stretched out and let himself pass out again.

When he opened his eyes another time, the colonel was sitting by his bedside reading a book. Giordano coughed softly and the colonel set his book aside. "You're in Tarrytown," Cross said. "You were shot in the course of the robbery. Do you remember it, Louis?"

"Yes."

"Are you hungry? Thirsty?"

"I don't think so. What time is it?"

"Twenty-three forty-five."

"Where is everybody?"

"In New Jersey. To rescue Edward."

"Just three of them? Jesus." He sat up, then winced at a spasm of pain from his leg. "You get the bullet out?"

"Yes. You were quite fortunate, incidentally. No bone damage and it missed the artery. It did nick a vein, so that you lost a bit of blood, but you should be ready to travel in a day or so. And you couldn't possibly have gone with them tonight. Don't even think of it."

"It'll be tough with three."

"I doubt it. They know the grounds and the placement of the guards and the procedure. I don't expect trouble."

"You don't look happy, sir."

"I'm not happy. I won't be happy until I learn Edward is all right." The colonel's face clouded. "The guard died," he said.

"Oh. Did I get him or was it Ben? My memory's a little spotty."

"It was Ben."

"Well."

The colonel sipped his drink. He was drinking Scotch and soda, and Giordano thought about Scotch and soda and decided that he didn't want anything at all just yet.

"The girl," he said suddenly.

"Sleeping. Helen gave her a sedative."

"I forgot all about her." He straightened up in the bed. "I could use a cigarette," he said.

"Right there on the table."

"Oh, right." He lit up and drew smoke into his lungs. "What do we do now?"

"She can't return to her former life, Louis. Witnesses reported that she recognized one of the holdup men and called him by name. And got the name wrong, believe it or not. She must have called you Jordan. The witnesses heard George."

"That's a break."

"Yes. But you see where we stand. She's in a position to give them full descriptions of all of us. Even if she were determined not to talk, the police wouldn't leave her alone."

"If she went away for a while until things cooled down——"

"We took that bank for almost a quarter of a million dollars. And as far as the police are concerned, we were also the ones who took the Passaic bank. They've made that much of the connection already, incidentally. By tomorrow they should know of Platt's relationship to both of the banks, which will dot the last *I* and cross the final *T*. In any case, they can only regard that girl as the sole key to two robberies in which three lives were lost. Things will never cool down, Louis."

"Then, what do we do with her?" The colonel didn't

say anything, and Giordano said, "No, I don't buy that. It's no good, sir."

"I didn't say anything yet, Louis."

"But what you didn't say was that we kill her, and no, sir, I just won't buy it."

"I haven't tried to sell it to you, Louis."

Giordano didn't seem to have heard. "The guard was something different. The guard was completely different. He was one of the soldiers on the other side, and on top of everything he was a schmuck who had to try and be a hero. It wasn't his money. It wasn't even that he was just doing his job. He must have run his ass off getting out the side and around the building in time to get himself killed. Screw the guard. And the bank VP that Frank shot, screw him too. He's a gangster. So the hell with him.

"But not the girl. If we start killing good people just because they're in the goddamned way, no, I'm sorry, sir, no, I don't like it."

The colonel was silent for a few minutes, and Giordano wondered if maybe he had talked too freely. He reviewed his words and decided he meant what he had said.

Cross said, "Would you rather marry her?"

"Her? Christ, no. I don't want to marry anybody. And not her. She's a good kid but nothing special. No, I don't want to marry her."

"It might be one or the other, Louis. Marry her or kill her, because the first law of nature has to be self-preservation."

"I know, but——"

"Even if you or I were willing to risk the consequences of releasing her, we couldn't do it. We have our responsibilities to the others."

"I know, sir."

"You'll want to give this some thought, Louis."

"Yes." He considered. "If I gave her a chunk of dough and let her run——"

"They'd pick her up in a week."

"I guess they would, sir."

Cross pushed his chair backward and pivoted to face the door. "I'll get out of your way for a while, Louis. Will you take something to eat now? Steak and eggs?"

"That does sound like a good idea."

"And a drink? Or would you rather have coffee?"

"I think coffee."

"Good." He paused at the door. "Louis? You ought to take your time thinking about this. See the girl before you decide. Sort out your own feelings."

"I'm sure as hell not going to marry her."

"Don't make any decision just now."

"So I guess we'll have to kill her, sir."

"You'll think it over, Louis."

Twenty-Seven

Simmons and Murdock went over the fence at the back of the Platt estate. Even with the current on, it wasn't a hard fence to get over. They hit the backyard at opposite sides and killed the three yard men in under five minutes. Simmons got two with a twenty-inch garotte of piano wire. Murdock used a knife on the other one.

When they encountered each other over the body of the third guard, Murdock cupped his hands and made a sound like an owl. When Dehn heard that he stood up from behind the bushes across the road and shot down the two guards at the front gate. He used a .22

rifle with a few yards of turkish towel wrapped around the barrel. The two shots still sounded like shots, but the noise didn't carry far enough to matter.

They left the garage alone. Manso had reported that no one lived in the rooms upstairs except for some of the servants, and cooks and cleaning women posed no great threat to them. They went to the backyard and played a pencil beam flashlight over the lawn. There were no traces of a fresh grave.

"He's in there," Dehn said. "He's alive. I feel it."

"You been going a lot by feelings lately."

"They've been working better for me than thought. Lately."

"Yeah. Burglar alarm feeds on household current?"

"Right."

Murdock wanted a look at it. When he saw the make, he told them it was no good. "Batteries cut in if the power cuts out. Eddie must not know how this model works, but I knew a boy in Chicago who went and bought himself five-to-ten in Joliet making the same old mistake. Cut the lines to the house and walked right on in and the alarm went off louder than a cat on barbed wire."

He checked the window glass in the house. There was tape around the perimeter of each pane, a silvery tape that was hooked into the alarm system, so that if you broke the window and the break ran through the tape, you would set off the alarm.

"But you can cut the glass," Murdock whispered. "Give me that whatchacallit, glass cutter."

When Manso heard footsteps, he moved behind the door and flattened out against the wall. He didn't know if it was day or night. He didn't know whose walk he heard or whether whoever it was was coming for him. He knew one thing only. If Platt opened that door, he was going to kill him the first chance he got.

He had his knife. They'd let him put his shoes on, and never noticed the little knife taped to the inner sole. He had it in his hand now. The footsteps were coming closer, and any second now there would be the sound of a key turning in the padlock, and the door would creak open, and Platt would come in, with or without a gun, with or without a bodyguard, and Platt was going to get a knife in his neck come hell or high water.

All day long the door had tempted him. It was wood, and thin, and its hinges were on the inside where he could get at them. All in all, it presented about as much of an obstacle as a fence to a bird. Even without the knife he could have gone through it in no time at all.

But what good would that do? If he busted out, the whole house would know about it. If he managed to take the damn thing off its hinges, he was still far from home free. The guards obviously had orders not to let him off the property, and it wouldn't be all that much of a cinch to break out of the place single-o.

So he had stayed where he was and he spent the day going through hell. Platt said he'd delivered his message to Helen Tremont, and if he did, the colonel would certainly be able to figure out which end was up, so there would be a rescue team coming in sooner or later. The question was just how long he could hold out. Sooner or later Platt would find someone who had known Florence Goddam Mannheim, and would prove conclusively that Eddie didn't exist.

He couldn't wait for Platt to let him know he'd got the news. He couldn't wait at all, as far as that went. Next time he had a shot at Platt, he would take it. If he got lucky, he'd find a way out afterward. If not, well, at least he'd take Platt along with him.

"Eddie? You down here, boy?"

"Ben!"

Footsteps coming close, and he lowered the knife and pressed up against the door.

"Ben?"

A low chuckle from Murdock. "Well, I've seen pris-

ons, you old son, but this here is positively escape-
proof. Why, this makes Alcatraz look like a day camp
for poor crippled kids."

"Open the door, will you?"

"Open it? Why, Eddie, there's a big old lock on it!
A wooden door with an actual padlock. Now, how in
the world can I go and open something like that?"

"Fuck you."

"Don't be nasty. I'm 'shamed of you, stuck behind a
little old wooden door." Manso heard the sound of
metal scraping, and then the door was drawn open.
Murdock was holding the padlock in his hand. Its
mountings hung from it. "Didn't even have to pick it
apart," he announced. "Silly thing came right up out of
the wood. Frank and Howard is upstairs. We did the
five outside and there was one on the first floor that I
almost fell over and still managed to cut him 'fore he
knew anybody was in the house."

"Where's Lou? And what about Platt?"

"Platt's upstairs, or leastwise I think it's him in a
room with a woman. We decided on finding you first
and lettin' you be in on it if you wanted. Lou, he got
shot in the laig. We took that bank, boy. You miss the
best part of things, don't you? Lou's okay. And the
team voted you a full share, even if you didn't get to
play in the World Series." His voice lost the lightness.
"You look sicker than a snake. You feeling poorly?"

"I caught a beating last night. I think it was last
night. But if you already took the bank—what the hell
time is it now?"

Murdock laughed. "You don't want to get all involved in details," he said. "Best to let your mind roll
on a bit. You come along with me now, boy, and we'll
go upstairs and kill Platt and get the hell out of here."

She was wearing a black bra and nothing else at all.
She sat at her dressing table brushing her dark hair.
Platt lay on the bed watching her. Anger mixed within
him with embryonic lust.

"Get over here," he said, "and get naked."

She turned and put the hairbrush down. "Aren't I naked enough, Albert?"

"Get outa the bra."

She reached behind her back to unhook the bra strap. He examined her critically. "They're starting to sag," he said. "Well, nothing lasts, does it? You get old and you sag a little."

"You son of a bitch."

"Get in bed."

She got in bed, but it was no good, nothing happened. After a few minutes he pushed her violently aside and sat up. She looked at him, eyes wide in surprise. This had not happened before.

"Well," she said, trying it on. "You get old and you sag a little, don't you?"

She expected an outburst, perhaps a slap. It didn't come. Instead he said, "You know the bank in New Cornwall? It got robbed."

"Was that the one? I heard something on the news."

"Yeah."

"So what? Did you have any money in it?"

He looked at her. "Oh, a little," he said.

"So you're insured, aren't you?"

He considered, then shrugged. "Right."

She got to her feet. He rolled over quickly, caught her arm, and pulled her down on the bed again. "You tell me the truth," he snapped. "You and Eddie. What happened?"

"It drives you crazy, doesn't it?"

"I don't like not knowing what's going on. Did he screw you?"

"Maybe."

"What shit is this?"

"Oh, maybe he did and maybe he didn't."

"You were pretty goddamned positive this morning."

"I guess I was at that. Albert, you're hurting me. Let go of my arm. I said let go."

"Bitch."

"What are you going to do?"

"To the kid? It depends."

"He's not your son, you know."

"What makes you so damn sure?"

"He told me."

"You're full of shit."

"No, he told me. He's a plant. Some of your friends in Chicago sent him to check up on you."

He sat up suddenly, his face white. Was somebody setting up some kind of power play? Kostakis had said he was getting a lot of static from South Jersey types who wanted in on the Trenton action. Maybe somebody on the council was setting up for a redistribution of wealth in Bergen County. And if they were getting ready for something like that, they were certainly maneuvering nicely. The shit with the bank was going to have cops on his neck night and day for weeks. And Buddy Rice was out of the way, and a Chicago plant was living in his house and screwing or not screwing his wife, depending on whether or not she was telling the truth—

That was the trouble. It all depended on whether or not she was telling the truth.

Because if you read it the other way, then the kid downstairs was his long-lost, goddamned son and the aggravation in New Cornwall was an accident, some punks who didn't know whose bank they were robbing, and all it meant was a few weeks of headaches for his lawyers.

But how in hell was he supposed to know what was true and what wasn't?

To himself as much as to her he said, "If I decide he's my kid, every time I look at him, I'm gonna wonder. All the time I'll be wondering. It's no good. Either he's lying or else his mother was crazy and gave him a crazy story. That dose I had, maybe it was just a dose, maybe all along I was sterile. Yeah, that's it. I could never have kids, so he couldn't be a kid of mine. Right?"

"If you say so, Albert."

"I say so."

"Are you going to kill him?"

"Well, I'll let him sweat until morning. And I'll let a couple of the boys open him up a little first. If there's anything in this Chicago thing."

"Don't you believe me?"

"Even if I did, which I don't, he could have been lying to you, kid."

"Oh."

He stretched out on the bed, pleased that things were working out, that the indecisiveness was gone. He reached out a hand and caught hold of one of her breasts. He squeezed sharply and she let out a bark of surprise.

"You got to expect sag with tits this size," he said. "Get over here. Open your legs, I want some."

"If you'll let me watch."

"Huh?"

"When you kill him."

"He gets to you, don't he?"

"Not what you think. Will you let me? I'll do it the way you always want."

He grinned and took her head in his hands. "You'll get a front-row seat," he told her.

He settled himself, closed his eyes, stroked her dark hair with his hands. "Oh, you bitch," he said softly, reverently. "Oh, you crazy, classy, screwed-up, delicious bitch. Oh, Jesus Christ."

Then the door flew open and Manso came in with a gun.

After

In the morning they spent long, lazy hours in bed. An hour or two past noon they would put on bathing suits and walk from their cabin to the beach twenty feet from their door. She never stayed in the water for any length of time. The Caribbean was a bright electric blue, always warm and always clear, with a clean sand bottom. He could swim in it for hours, and sometimes did. She would go in with him and paddle around for a few minutes. Then she would go ashore and lie down on their blanket under the sun. Like him, she tanned readily and did not burn, and within a week she was brown.

At night after dinner they would usually stick around the lodge for a couple of hours. The native bartender did clever things with rum, and the owner, an Alsatian Jew with one blue eye and one brown eye, would join them at their table and trade lies with them.

Then a midnight swim, and lovemaking, and sleep.

She said, "I wish we could stay here forever."

"Nothing's forever."

"I know."

"And the secret is not to stay any one place too long. That's one of the secrets."

"And the other is never come back, because no place is ever as good the second time around."

"How did you know? Oh, that's right, I made this speech before, didn't I?"

"Yes."

"You look good as a blonde."

"I'll have to get to a beauty parlor. The roots are starting to show."

"I didn't notice. The blond hair and the tan—I don't think your own mother would recognize you."

"Well, we can't test that out, can we?"

"No, I'm afraid we can't." He started to say something else, then changed direction. "I called the airport. I booked us on a Trans-Carib flight Thursday to Miami. Then from there we fly Delta. We could have had a through flight Wednesday on Pan Am, but the Trans-Carib's a better line. And this way we have an extra day."

"I'm glad of that. Will I like Phoenix?"

"I like it. And you can keep the tan year-round out there."

"Will you . . . still want me in Phoenix?"

"Of course."

"I mean, I figured there were other girls there."

"Nothing serious."

"Because you and I have no strings. I'm alive, that's enough. If you see something you want——"

"We'll just keep on keeping on, huh?"

"Because what you said—nothing's forever."

Later: "I wonder where they all are, what they're doing."

"The colonel's reading something. His Bible or some military history. Helen's probably baking. The others? Howard was going to spend a couple of days in New York. There were some stamp auctions he wanted to go to. Frank is on the road somewhere, I don't know where. Ben's probably in the drunk tank of some jail or other. He generally goes on a bender afterwards and drinks up all his money."

"How can anybody drink up fifty thousand dollars?"

"Ben would try, but he doesn't have to. If he took all his cash he'd get himself in all kinds of trouble. He generally takes a thousand or two. He keeps five hundred bucks for getaway money and blows the rest. What he doesn't take, the colonel invests for him. Ben must be worth, oh, a quarter of a million."

"You would never guess it."

"He doesn't act it. He doesn't even think about it, which is why he manages to stay out of trouble. You see, that's the whole thing, you have to create a life for yourself that you feel comfortable in. Like we could spend absolutely all our time traveling and living it up, but then life would just be something in between the jobs, and it's harder to live that way. Same with Ben. When he runs out of dough, he'll get a job somewhere. And live like a bum until the colonel gives him a call."

"And Eddie? He's in Europe?"

He nodded. "Monte Carlo, I think. He wants to stay away from the stateside gambling areas, at least for the time being. He's clean as far as the police are concerned, but he figures it might be good to let the gambling types have some time to forget about Platt and his wife. You want to go in for a minute before we go back to the cabin?"

"I don't think so."

"I'll just take a dip, then. It seems to be doing my leg some good."

She sat on the beach and watched him bobbing in the waves. She lit a cigarette, then poked the burnt match into the sand.

She would not see her children again, or her parents. Perhaps not ever, and certainly not for many years.

She thought that there must be something wrong with her. Because she had loved the children, and she had cared for her mother and father, and now she was never going to see them again and she didn't seem to care at all. It seemed unnatural, and she thought that there must be something wrong with her.

She was tan, she was blond, she glowed with health and vitality. She was eating like a horse and still losing weight, slimming down nicely. And her face, when she caught sight of it in a mirror, looked back at her radiant with the joy of being alive and in love.

He didn't want to get married. Well, neither did she, because he was right and nothing was forever. Sooner or later he would probably want to be rid of her. He denied this now, but she expected it would happen sooner or later. But by then she would be trained in a new life role, and she wouldn't go back to New Jersey and the police would never find her.

According to the papers, she was presumed dead. A hostage, kidnapped and presumed dead. Well, she thought, so be it. Patricia Novak, rest in peace. Patricia Crosby, welcome to the club.

Giordano was emerging from the surf. He walked easily, hardly favoring the leg at all. She looked at him in the moonlight and her blood quickened, and she ran across the sand to meet him.